PRAISE FOR THE BOOK

The fact that William Shakespeare is considered one of the greatest playwrights of all time does not necessarily make him a favourite of English literature students, even in the land of his birth. It often takes a gifted teacher to illuminate his greatness and reveal the depths and range of his humanity and explain the often complicated plots. If this does not happen, it is unlikely that the uninspired will ever read one of his plays in later life. If they are fortunate, they will see one of them performed by actors well versed in every nuance. If they see one of his comedies, *A Midsummer Night's Dream*, for instance, they will be surprised to find themselves convulsed with laughter. If they then see more plays, they will soon understand his extraordinary range and genius, that he was a master of not only comedy, but of history and tragedy.

DEEPTI MENON has done a great service to those whose schools' syllabuses include Shakespeare. While the worlds he wrote about are unfamiliar to students and his turns of phrase are no longer in vogue, his characters play out their roles in complex plots. Now students can at least unravel these complexities and use her clearly written book to become familiar with the story and characters each play contains. In each play, she has included a handful of quotes, not only providing a sample of his words, but often surprising us with phrases we never knew were Shakespeare's. Her sentences are unburdened with confusion or unnecessary elaboration, the flow of the stories enabling the reader to navigate the choppy seas of Shakespeare's greatness, making him accessible, understood, and appreciated.

PEPITA SETH
Padma Shri Awardee, Author, Photographer

CLASSIC TALES

FROM

SHAKESPEARE

DEEPTI MENON

READO JUNIOR

Reado Junior, an imprint of Readomania Publishing
A division of Kurious Kind Media Private Limited
readomania.com
Email: contact@readomania.com
Facebook: facebook.com/iamreadomania
Twitter: twitter.com/iamreadomania
Instagram: iamreadomania

First Published in 2023 by Reado Junior, an imprint
of Readomania

Edited by Indrani Ganguly (Managing Editor, Readomania)

ISBN: 978-93-91800-56-7

Typeset in Palatino Linotype by Shine Graphics
Printed in New Delhi

READO JUNIOR

*"A person who won't read has no advantage over
one who can't read."*

—*Mark Twain.*

The Internet has revolutionized our world. For many of us, a large part of our day is spent online. Even the entertainment options are on digital platforms. The world needs alternatives. So why not reading?

Like Frank Serafini said, "There is no such thing as a child who hates to read; there are only children who have not found the right book." So, we take the responsibility to provide the best books for you, our young readers, in your favourite genres, under READO JUNIOR. Our content is based on the FREEDOM principle: **F**un, **R**elevant, **E**ngaging, **E**ntertaining, and **DOM**inant. It is the kind of content that will give the reader freedom from the digital medium. The narration in READO JUNIOR titles matches your age-specific lexical and cognitive ability, supported by illustrations and attractive layouts to entice book lovers like you.

Our logo shows the Reado Swan, a representation of knowledge and wisdom, that can fly to the stars. The Reado Swan represents you, our reader, who gains knowledge and wisdom through our books to dream big and reach the stars.

Join us in this movement to make reading a habit and good books a part of our lives.

CONTENTS

A NOTE ON WILLIAM SHAKESPEARE

(23rd April, 1564–23rd April, 1616)

'All the world's a stage,
And all the men and women merely players;
They have their exits and their entrances;
And one man in his time plays many parts,
His acts being seven ages.'

Jacques—*As You Like It*

In the vast canvas of English literature, the one name that stands out like a beacon, throwing light over his contemporaries, is that of William Shakespeare. Not for nothing is he referred to as England's national poet and the Bard of Avon.

Stratford-upon-Avon basks in reflected glory. William was born there in 1564 to John Shakespeare and Mary Arden, the third of their eight children. He attended the King's New School and was imparted intensive education of the grammar based on Latin classical authors, a fact that certainly influenced his writings later in life.

At the age of 18, William met Anne Hathaway, eight years older than he was, and his life changed. As someone said jokingly, 'Anne "hath her way" and she married William.' They had three children—Susanna, and the twins Hamnet and Judith.

The Elizabethan era saw the Renaissance of art and literature. Shakespeare burst onto the scene with two long poems. He was one of the founding members of a theatre troupe called The Chamberlain's Men, which went on to stage many of his plays.

What a glorious career it was, as he did 'strut his way across the stage' creating magic all the way!

Shakespeare wrote 38 plays, 2 narrative poems, 154 sonnets (14-line poems) and numerous other poems. None of the original manuscripts are available today. Luckily, a group of players who performed the plays compiled around 36 of his plays and published them in the First Folio. The world owes them a debt of gratitude for this. Shakespeare also created a historical space which was aptly named The Globe Theatre, and even today, thousands of tourists flock to it to experience how it felt to view drama during his time.

Why is Shakespeare still being read, his plays enacted? How many adaptations of his works have found niches for themselves, be it in movies, books or theatre? Hundreds of titles of books, plays, musicals and films have been adapted from Shakespearean quotes: *The Sound and The Fury* by William Faulkner, *Under the Greenwood Tree* by Thomas Hardy, *Brave New World* by Aldous Huxley, *North by Northwest* by Alfred Hitchcock, *The Moon is Down* by John Steinbeck, *Something Wicked This Way Comes* by Ray Bradbury and even the popular *The Fault in Our Stars* by John Green.

There are so many phrases and adages that are in common parlance, thrown around so carelessly, but few know that they originated from Shakespeare's prolific pen. For example, 'all that glitters is not gold', 'the be-all and end-all', 'the world's my oyster', 'as luck would have it', 'neither a borrower nor a lender be', 'wild goose chase' and many more.

Shakespeare's plays were grand spectacles, but there were concepts that appealed both to the rich and the poor. They held a mirror up to life, often incorporating elements of magic, romance, passion and philanthropy, on one hand, and the baser emotions like envy, greed, ambition, and hatred on the other. His was a vast canvas populated by kings and queens, princes and princesses, merchants and money lenders, spirits and fairies, lovers and enemies. His tragedies had heroes with fatal flaws, his comedies encapsulated the philosophy of life often pronounced by fools and jesters who were wiser than the wisest.

As Shakespeare grew older, his plays also followed a natural progression from historical themes, like *Richard III* and *Henry IV, V* and *VI*, to more playful ones, like *A Midsummer Night's Dream, Much Ado About Nothing, The Merchant of Venice* and *Twelfth Night*.

It was closer to the autumn of his life that his tragic plays like *Macbeth, Hamlet, Othello, Coriolanus* and *King Lear* were written. These were considered his triumphs and have been staged more often than any of his earlier works. His sonnets were intensely personal, often revealing Shakespeare's views on topics like life, love, religion and marriage.

If there is one towering figure that has influenced many personages like Charles Dickens, Herman Melville, Agatha Christie and Anthony Burgess, it is the Bard. His influence has also been felt in the realms of music and art, opera and psychology.

A Note on William Shakespeare

As Cassius remarked to Brutus in Julius Caesar:

'Why, man, he doth bestride the narrow world
Like a Colossus, and we petty men
Walk under his huge legs and peep about
To find ourselves dishonourable graves.'

He could as well have been lauding Shakespeare for having been the most spectacular playwright and man of letters of the time, and beyond, even till the present day.

This book contains ten stories adapted from the original plays of William Shakespeare, in chronological order. As the author and adaptor, I have 'attempted' to narrate these classic stories in a way that may be intelligible and interesting to the younger generation, children between the ages of ten and seventeen. Of course, this is merely a surmise. The stories are out there for all those who love Shakespeare and his storytelling, and that is the reason why I have retained a few lines from the original texts so that the reader may savour a tentative taste of the language, and hopefully, go on to make a full meal of it.

The stories have been chosen with care because, to carry on the above metaphor, reading Shakespeare is like sampling a buffet, where there are so many dishes that unless chosen judiciously, might lead the taster on to indigestion. For that very reason, I have combined tragedy and comedy with history so that there is a hint of every flavour and a surfeit of none. I do hope, from the bottom of my heart, that I have succeeded in my task.

If not, let me apologize and end with the words of Robin Goodfellow (the lovable Puck) from *A Midsummer Night's Dream*:

A Note on William Shakespeare

'If we shadows have offended,
Think but this, and all is mended,
That you have but slumbered here
While these visions did appear.
And this weak and idle theme,
No more yielding but a dream,
Gentles, do not reprehend:
If you pardon, we will mend:
And, as I am an honest Puck,
If we have unearned luck
Now to 'scape the serpent's tongue,
We will make amends ere long;
Else the Puck a liar call;
So, good night unto you all.
Give me your hands, if we be friends,
And Robin shall restore amends.'

DEEPTI MENON
Thrissur, 2023

1

THE TWO GENTLEMEN OF VERONA

1.1: *The Two Gentlemen of Verona.*
Artist: Manasa Kalyan.

Characters in the Order of their Appearance

Proteus, a gentleman of Verona
Valentine, also a gentleman of Verona
Julia/Sebastian, Proteus's first lady love

Speed, Valentine's man servant
Lance, Proteus' man servant
Lucetta, Julia's maid
Antonio, Proteus's father
The Duke of Milan
Silvia, the Duke's daughter
Lord Thurio, Silvia's suitor
A Gang of Outlaws
Lord Eglamour, a supposedly gallant young man

Proteus and Valentine, the two gentlemen of Verona, were close friends who viewed life in different ways. Valentine was all agog to see the world outside Verona, and hence, he planned to visit Milan to seek adventure and honour. Proteus, on the other hand, preferred to stay in Verona because he was in love with the beautiful Julia and hoped to woo her. When the day arrived for Valentine to leave, the two friends bid each other an emotional farewell, promising to stay in touch. Valentine bade farewell to his friend with the words,

'Sweet Proteus, no; now let us take our leave.
To Milan let me hear from thee by letters
Of thy success in love.'

Valentine entreated Proteus to send him letters describing his success in love.

Once Valentine had left, his man servant, Speed, hurried in, looking for his master. Proteus asked him if he had delivered his love letter to Julia. Speed replied that he had, and that Julia had merely nodded and not responded in any other manner.

Proteus asked him what his lady love had conveyed. Speed's reply was brief.

'Sir, I could perceive nothing at all from her; no,
not so much as a ducat for delivering your letter.'

Proteus was downcast and rued that he had sent his precious letter through such a worthless messenger.

Speed had delivered Proteus's letter to Lucetta, Julia's maid. When Julia asked Lucetta which of her suitors she should choose, Lucetta spoke of Proteus, which surprised her mistress as she had no idea that he loved her because he was a man of few words. Lucetta confessed that she had accepted a letter addressed to Julia from Valentine's man, Speed. Julia chastised her and sent her away, but immediately called her back. However, the two exchanged words and irked, Julia tore the letter into shreds. Once Lucetta had left the room, Julia picked up the pieces and tried to read the words of love from Proteus on it, proving that she was also in love with him. She lamented that she had treated his letter so unkindly, exclaiming,

'I'll kiss each several paper for amends.'

Antonio, Proteus's father, was concerned that his son was spending too much time at home when he should have been travelling the world, learning the graces of a young gentleman. Having learnt that Valentine had gone to Milan to attend on the Duke, Antonio decided that Proteus too would follow suit the very next day. Just then, an ecstatic Proteus walked in, reading a letter from Julia which expressed her willingness to marry him. When his father quizzed him about the letter, he lied, stating that it was from Valentine describing the wonderful time he was having.

'There is no news, my lord, but that he writes
How happily he lives, how well beloved
And daily graced by the emperor;
Wishing me with him, partner of his fortune.'

This pleased Antonio who ordered his son to make his way to Milan so that he could spend time with Valentine at the Duke's court.

Valentine had, by now, lost his heart to the charming Silvia, the Duke's daughter. Silvia had requested him to write a love letter for her, one that she wanted to send to a secret nameless friend. Valentine did so with reluctance. She chided him for making it so scholarly, and gave it back to him, indicating that the letter was meant for him, a fact that Valentine took time to understand.

Proteus and Julia met, vowing that they would stay true to each other. Julia offered him a ring as a keepsake. Julia entreated him to keep her in his heart.

'Keep this remembrance for thy Julia's sake.'

He, in turn, offered her his ring, vowing that it would remind her of his love for her. He then left for Milan. Proteus's manservant, Lance, dragged his surly dog, Crab, to the departing ship, lamenting that the dog showed no sorrow at being parted from his master.

When Proteus reached Milan, Valentine was elated to see him and introduced him to Silvia. Once Silvia was out of earshot, Valentine confessed his love for her, calling her the most divine beauty ever. He added to his friend that he and she planned to elope that very night. Proteus disagreed with Valentine about Silvia's beauty, but secretly, he too had fallen in love with her. His love for Julia had been driven out by his stronger love for

Silvia, which made him forget his love for his old friend, Valentine.

> *'At first I did adore a twinkling star,*
> *But now I worship a celestial sun.'*

He was aware that if he chose Silvia, he would lose both Julia and his dear friend, Valentine.

> *'Julia I lose and Valentine I lose:*
> *If I keep them, I needs must lose myself.'*

So enamoured was he by Silvia that he decided that he would inform the Duke, her father, of Valentine's secret plan to climb to Silvia's chamber window with a corded ladder to help her to elope with him. While his unfaithful mind was plotting thus, back home, Julia missed him desperately. She decided to disguise herself as a page named Sebastian and make her way to Milan to find Proteus, secure in her belief that he loved her.

> *'His words are bonds, his oaths are oracles,*
> *His love sincere, his thoughts immaculate.*
> *His tears pure messengers sent from his heart,*
> *His heart as far from fraud as heaven from earth.'*

The Duke was eager to have Silvia marry Lord Thurio, a man of wealth. He had a tiny suspicion that Silvia and Valentine were in love. Thus, when Proteus disclosed the plot of their elopement, he was enraged. The false Proteus added fuel to the fire.

> *'Know, worthy prince, Sir Valentine, my friend,*
> *This night intends to steal away your daughter.'*

Proteus requested the Duke not to mention his name in connection with the plot. The Duke accosted Valentine and slyly got the whole plot out of him, including a letter that the latter had written to Silvia mentioning that he would abduct her that very night. The Duke banished him from his court immediately. Valentine was desperate because he could not face life without Silvia by his side.

'What light is light, if Silvia be not seen?
What joy is joy, if Silvia be not by?'

The cunning Proteus advised him to leave Milan as his life was in danger. He assured him that he would pass on Valentine's letters to his lady love.

'Time is the nurse and breeder of all good.
Here if thou stay, thou canst not see thy love.'

Once Valentine was safely out of the way, Proteus ordered his servant, Lance, to offer a lapdog as a gift to Silvia. The lapdog disappeared and Lance substituted it with the high-spirited Crab, but the dog behaved so atrociously that the gesture backfired on him.

Silvia was heartbroken after Valentine left. She spurned the advances of Lord Thurio, the suitor chosen for her by her father. The Duke asked Proteus to slander Valentine in front of Silvia so that she would fall out of love with Valentine and turn to Lord Thurio instead. Proteus advised Lord Thurio to turn more romantic and pursue Sylvia with music and poetry.

'Say that upon the altar of her beauty
You sacrifice your tears, your sighs, your heart.'

A dispirited Valentine and his servant, Speed, wandered through a forest on the outskirts of Mantua when they were accosted by a gang of outlaws. The outlaws asked Valentine many questions. When they heard that he had been banished from Milan, they asked him to join them as their general for he was a presentable young man who would bring credit to their gang. Valentine accepted because he had nothing more than the clothes on his back, his only condition being that the gang would not waylay women or poor travellers.

Meanwhile, Sir Thurio had arranged a group of musicians to serenade Silvia and Julia, in the guise of Sebastian, had accompanied them. Once the song was over, she heard Proteus assure Sir Thurio that he would speak to the fair lady and plead the latter's suit. Sir Thurio and the musicians left soon after.

Proteus then spoke of his own love for Silvia, but she berated him, calling him disloyal and false. She told him to return to his lady love, but Proteus claimed that she was dead, much to the dismay of Julia who was a silent listener. Silvia spoke of her love for Valentine, a love that would bury itself in his grave if he were to die. Proteus requested her to give him a picture of hers that was hanging in her chamber. Disgusted, Silvia gave in and said that she would give him her picture, but never would she be his idol. The disguised Julia was heartbroken as she sighed,

> *'It hath been the longest night*
> *That ere I watch'd and the most heaviest.'*

Silvia had made up her mind that she would go to Mantua to look for Valentine. She called for Lord Eglamour, a gallant young man, to escort her through the perilous forests. She had faith in him as he was aware that the Duke was trying to force her to marry a man she did not love. He consented to go along with her that evening.

Proteus and Julia, disguised as Sebastian, came in together. Proteus gave Sebastian a ring, mentioning that it was from one who had loved him. He wanted Sebastian to give it to Silvia along with a letter and ask her for the picture that she had promised him. Sebastian (Julia) was hurt at the indifference with which Proteus mentioned her. He remarked that he pitied the poor abandoned lady.

> *'Because methinks that she loved you as well*
> *As you do love your lady Silvia:*
> *She dreams of him that has forgot her love;*
> *You dote on her that cares not for your love.*
> *'Tis pity love should be so contrary.'*

After Proteus left, she perceived Silvia, and handed over the letter to her. Reluctant to take it, Silvia tore it up. Julia, as Sebastian, took the opportunity to talk about herself, the woman who loved Proteus. She added that Julia was overwrought to hear that he had shifted his affections to another. Silvia sympathized with Julia's plight and presented the young page with the picture she had promised Proteus and a purse of money for Sebastian's loyalty to Julia. The heartbroken Julia thanked Silvia for her kindness.

> *'I thank you, madam, that you tender her.*
> *Poor gentlewoman! my master wrongs her much.'*

By then, the Duke had realized that Silvia had fled with Sir Eglamour and was on her way to meet Valentine. He, Proteus, Thurio and Sebastian made haste to follow on their heels. Silvia was captured by the outlaws who took her to their chief. Meanwhile, Proteus and Julia too reached there. Proteus continued to speak of his love for Silvia, which Valentine heard, unseen. When Proteus finally tried to force his suit on Silvia, Valentine came to her rescue, denouncing Proteus as a false friend.

'Proteus, I am sorry I must never trust thee more,
But count the world a stranger for thy sake.'

However, in an instant, Proteus turned repentant, and Valentine accepted him as his friend again. He told him that he could have Silvia for his wife.

When Julia heard this, she fainted. After she recovered, she revealed the ring that Proteus had asked her to present to Silvia. When Proteus saw the ring, he was taken aback because it was the ring that he had given Julia when he left her. Julia then revealed her identity and Proteus came back to his senses. He realized that he was still in love with her.

There was a commotion outside as the outlaws brought in two captives—the Duke and Thurio. Thurio claimed Silvia as his, but Valentine silenced him with a threat, after which he gave up his claim on her. The Duke applauded his spirit and repealed his banishment with these words,

'Sir Valentine,
Thou are a gentleman and well derived;
Take thou thy Silvia, for thou hast deserved her.'

Valentine had one boon to ask of the Duke. He requested him to forgive the outlaws their offences for they were all worthy men, reformed and fit for employment, a request that was readily accepted by the Duke.

'These banish'd men that I have kept withal
Are men endued with worthy qualities:
Forgive them what they have committed here
And let them be recall'd from their exile.'

As they walked along, Valentine told the Duke about the love story of Proteus and his Julia, adding in the end that both the gentlemen of Verona, Valentine and Proteus, would be married on the same day to their lady loves. Generous as ever, he remarked to Proteus,

'Our day of marriage shall be yours;
One feast, one house, one mutual happiness.'

Brief Note

The Two Gentlemen of Verona, written between 1590 and 1594, is believed to be one of the earliest plays by Shakespeare. Also considered a pastoral story, it was published in the First Folio of 1623. Many critics have remarked on the immaturity of this play as compared to his later ones. This was also one of his simplest plays with a small cast of characters, and the first play to show a woman dressed as a man, a motif that he carried on in many of his other productions as well. The themes follow the natural progression of friendship and betrayal, the conflict between love and loyalty and the follies that people in love commit.

The play falls into the category of tragicomedy, with elements of both tragedy and comedy in it. However, there is no great passion revealed by any of the characters, one of whom constantly falls in and out of love. There are moments of humour in the play especially displayed by the two manservants, Speed and Lance, especially when the latter talks about the 'ungentlemanly' behaviour of Crab, his dog. In fact, only two animals appear in any of the Bard's plays—Crab, the dog, in *The Two Gentlemen of Verona* and a nameless hungry bear in *The Winter's Tale*. However, due to his unruly nature, Crab has been immortalised as the only canine in a Shakespearean play.

2

THE TAMING OF THE SHREW

2.1: *The Taming of the Shrew.*
Artist: Pavithra S. Nair.

Characters in the Order of their Appearance

The Lord
Christopher Sly
Bartholomew

Lucentio/Gambio
Tranio
Baptista Minola
Katherine
Bianca
Hortensio/Licio
Gremio
Biondello
Petruchio
Grumio
The Wealthy Widow
The False Vincentio
Vincentio

There was once a Lord who came across a man named Christopher Sly in a tavern on the English countryside. Sly had broken a few glasses, quarrelled with the hostess of the ale house and then passed out. The Lord decided to have some fun with the drunk tinker. He ordered his men to carry Sly to his home, dress him up in finery, adorn his fingers with rings and feed him with delicacies.

> *'Sirs, I will practise on this drunken man.*
> *What think you, if he were convey'd to bed,*
> *Wrapp'd in sweet clothes, rings put upon his fingers,*
> *A most delicious banquet by his bed,*
> *And brave attendants near him when he wakes,*
> *Would not the beggar then forget himself?'*

They were to treat him like a lord who had recovered from his insanity over the past fifteen years. He also ordered his young page, Bartholomew, to disguise himself as Sly's wife and pretend to be the lady of the house.

Just then, a troupe of players arrived there. The Lord asked them to entertain the man, all the while putting on a straight face and treating him as a lord.

The troupe played their parts well, including the Lord himself who pretended to be a servant. Finally, Christopher Sly was convinced that he was a lord who had a lady wife. Together they would watch the play put on by the above-mentioned players.

The play opened in the city of Padua where Lucentio had come along with his servant, Tranio. Lucentio was an erudite young man educated in Florence and Pisa, who wanted to further his learning at the University of Padua. As they talked, they were interrupted by a commotion. Baptista Minola, a wealthy man, came in with his two daughters, Katherine and Bianca. They were followed by two older men, Hortensio and Gremio, who were both in love with Bianca, the gentle younger daughter of Baptista.

However, Baptista told them firmly that until his elder daughter, Katherine, was married, he would not allow his second daughter to be courted by anyone. He added that both could woo Katherine instead.

'Gentlemen, importune me no farther,
For how I firmly am resolved you know;
That is, not bestow my youngest daughter
Before I have a husband for the elder.'

Katherine was an ill-tempered and surly girl who had no control over her tongue. The two suitors backed off saying that no one would dare marry a devil like Katherine, even as she shouted at them. While this was going on, Lucentio kept gazing on the mild and sober younger girl, Bianca. Bianca was distressed by the situation. She said that she would busy herself in her musical instruments and her books instead of thinking of marriage.

While Katherine railed on, Bianca left the room. Baptista instructed the two suitors to find a schoolmaster to teach Bianca. Left alone, the two suitors put their heads together and agreed that they either needed to find a husband for Katherine or a teacher for Bianca.

Meanwhile, Lucentio had lost his heart to Bianca.

'Tranio, I burn, I pine, I perish, Tranio,
If I achieve not this young modest girl.'

Tranio mentioned Katherine who had raised such a storm and scolded all the men around. However, it was clear that Lucentio had noticed nothing but the beautiful Bianca. Tranio realized that it was time to wake his young master out of his trance. He said,

'Her eldest sister is so curst and shrewd
That till the father rid his hands of her,
Master, your love must live a maid at home.'

Lucentio remarked that he would dress up as a school master and tutor Bianca in the hope that he would be able to win her heart, while his servant, Tranio, would pretend to be Lucentio and attend the university. Biondello, the other servant of Lucentio, was also drawn into the deception.

It was time for Petruchio, the fearless hero of the story, to make an appearance along with Grumio, his servant. Petruchio had come from Verona to Padua to visit his old friend, Hortensio, who was elated to see him. He asked Petruchio,

'And tell me now, sweet friend, what happy gale
Blows you to Padua here from old Verona?'

Petruchio mentioned that his father had died and now, he was set to find himself a rich wife.

'Antonio, my father, is deceased;
And I have thrust myself into this maze,
Haply to wive and thrive as best I may:
Crowns in my purse I have and goods at home,
And so am come abroad to see the world.'

Hortensio's quick mind went to Katherine who was rich, though shrewish, and he mentioned her to Petruchio, warning him about her bad temper.

'I can, Petruchio, help thee to a wife
With wealth enough and young and beauteous,
Brought up as best becomes a gentlewoman:
Her only fault, and that is faults enough,
Is that she is intolerable curst
And shrewd and froward.'

All Petruchio wanted was a rich wife and he asked Hortensio to lead him to her. When he heard the name of Baptista Minola, he said that his father had known the gentleman, and so did he.

There were now four suitors for Bianca's hand. Lucentio, who was disguised as a schoolmaster, Tranio who was dressed as Lucentio, Hortensio who was in the garb of a music master and Gremio, the elderly suitor, who had no idea that Lucentio had also fallen in love with her, which meant that he himself had no chance with her. When the others heard that Petruchio was prepared to woo Katherine, all the suitors made their way to Baptista's house the next day.

Chaos ensued as Katherine, who had tied Bianca's hands together, chased her in a fury to find out which of the suitors she liked.

'Of all thy suitors, here I charge thee, tell
Whom thou lovest best: see thou dissemble not.'

When Bianca refused to tell her, she beat her, trying to get an answer out. Baptista came to his younger daughter's rescue, which only angered her more because she felt that he was partial to Bianca. She flounced out in a rage.

Petruchio made an appearance at Baptista's house. He described himself as a young gentleman from Verona.

'Petruchio is my name; Antonio's son,
A man well known throughout all Italy.'

He had come there on the pretext of having heard many good things about Katherine.

'I am a gentleman of Verona, sir,
That, hearing of her beauty and her wit,
Her affability and bashful modesty,
Her wondrous qualities and mild behaviour,
Am bold to show myself a forward guest
Within your house.'

He presented Hortensio as a master skilled in mathematics and music, calling him Licio.

An impatient Gremio interrupted him to present Baptista with the gift of a young scholar, Cambio, who was Lucentio in disguise, as a scholar well versed in Greek, Latin and other languages.

Baptista then turned to Tranio and asked him what the purpose of his visit was. Tranio introduced himself as Lucentio, the son of Vincentio of Pisa. He claimed to be a suitor to Bianca and presented Baptista with a gift of Greek and Latin books, as also a lute, for his daughters.

Baptista welcomed all the gifts and despatched the fake tutors with a servant to meet his daughters. Petruchio reminded Baptista of his suit and asked him about the dowry that Katherine would bring with her. Baptista answered that she would have one half of his properties and twenty thousand crowns after his death.

'After my death the one half of my lands,
And in possession twenty thousand crowns.'

Petruchio assured him that he too would maintain her in style and suggested that they draw up a mutual agreement. When Baptista said that Petruchio needed to gain Katherine's love first, he answered that that would be no problem.

'Why, that is nothing: for I tell you, father,
I am as peremptory as she proud-minded;
And where two raging fires meet together
They do consume the thing that feeds their fury.'

Just then, Hortensio came in, bleeding as Katherine had hit him over the head with the lute and called him names. This amused Petruchio and made him eager to meet her.

When Katherine walked in and began to rail at him, Petruchio called her Kate and the two sparred, using puns and verbal barbs against each other. Katherine lost her temper and struck him, which only made him keener to marry her and tame her rough temper.

'Thou must be married to no man but me;
For I am he am born to tame you, Kate,
And bring you from a wild Kate to a Kate
Conformable as other household Kates.'

When Baptista came in again, Petruchio told him that he had wooed Kate and that they had decided that their wedding would be on Sunday. Surprisingly, Katherine did not react and hence, the date was fixed. Petruchio would go to Venice and buy the rings for the wedding.

Once Petruchio and Katherine exited, Gremio and Tranio sparred over who would wed Bianca. Baptista promised her hand to the one who offered her the bigger dowry. Tranio, as Lucentio, seemed to have more to offer and hence, Baptista agreed to give Bianca's hand in marriage to him.

Meanwhile, Lucentio and Hortensio, both in disguise, attempted to woo Bianca through their respective talents.

The day of the wedding dawned and Baptista, Katherine and all the guests were waiting for the tardy bridegroom outside Baptista's house. As time went by, Katherine lost patience and ran into the house shedding petulant tears. Baptista had also begun to fret when he heard that Petruchio was on his way, along with his servant. They were both dressed in shabby, mismatched clothes, riding on old diseased horses.

Petruchio strode in and Baptista was horrified at his appearance. He requested him to change his apparel, saying,

> *'Why, sir, you know this is your wedding day:*
> *First were we sad, fearing you would not come:*
> *Now sadder, that you come so unprovided.'*

Petruchio refused to change his clothes for better ones and set off to the church in a rush to see his beautiful Kate. He behaved atrociously during the wedding. He swore so loudly that the priest dropped his book, and when he bent down to pick it up, Petruchio hit him on his head.

He demanded wine and threw food around. Luckily, the wedding was conducted, and the guests were expected back soon.

A grand wedding feast was prepared, and yet, Petruchio was in a hurry to get home. Even though Katherine entreated him to stay for the feast, he refused. Katherine lost her temper and told him that he could go, but that she would only move when she wanted to. She invited the guests to her wedding feast, remarking,

'I see a woman may be made a fool,
If she had not a spirit to resist.'

Petruchio retorted that she was now his property as she was wed to him. He pretended that Kate needed defending from thieves and asked his servant to draw his weapon. Thus saying, he hurried away with Kate, while the amused guests laughed at the strange events that had ensued.

Kate was in for a rude shock ahead. After a tiring journey, where she fell off the horse into the slushy mud, she went into her new home, hoping for a warm meal. However, Petruchio misbehaved once more, screaming at his men servants who had assembled to greet the new bride. He accused them of not attending on him. When supper was brought in, he claimed that the mutton was burnt, and he threw it on the floor. When Kate tried to remonstrate with him, he assured her that everything had to be perfect for his new bride and that they would fast that night. He pretended not to notice that all she wanted was a hot meal.

Petruchio had a plan up his sleeve. He was behaving thus on purpose because he wanted to tame his new wife who was like a wild falcon. He intended to keep her off balance by complaining about the bed, the sheets and the pillows, so that she would not be able to sleep. If she did nod off, he would clamour and keep her awake.

> *'This is a way to kill a wife with kindness:*
> *And thus back I'll curb her mad and headstrong humour.'*

Back in Padua, Hortensio had watched the schoolmaster wooing Bianca and he decided that he would give up his claim on her and marry a wealthy widow instead.

Lucentio now needed someone to impersonate his father, Vincentio of Pisa, and assure his future father in law of a generous dowry. He managed to coerce an aged scholar from Mantua to do so. The nervous old man met Baptista, and the two decided that Lucentio and Bianca would be wed. An unsuspecting Baptista was now confronted with a double deception, a fake Lucentio and his counterfeit father. They all went to a private place to discuss the details of the wedding.

Meanwhile, at Petruchio's home, Kate's troubles had just begun. She was still hungry, and she entreated Grumio, the servant, to fetch her something to eat. He mentioned all kinds of meats but refrained from bringing her anything. She was both irritable and exhausted.

> *'But I, who never knew how to entreat,*
> *Nor never needed that I should entreat,*
> *Am starved for meat, giddy for lack of sleep.'*

Petruchio brought her a meal, but before she could eat it, a tailor entered with a fashionable gown for her to wear when they visited Padua next. Petruchio found fault with the gown, and the cap with it, and he sent the tailor away in a fury.

Kate was angry and spoke her mind but Petruchio deflected what she said by assuring her that their poor garments did not define them.

> *'Even in these honest mean habiliments:*
> *Our purses shall be proud, our garments poor;*
> *For 'tis the mind that makes the body rich.'*

He changed the topic by telling her that they would go back to her father's house to feast and sport there before noon. Kate contradicted him, pointing out that it was already past noon. This annoyed him and he accused her of crossing him and cancelled the plan. They would go the next day instead.

> *'I will not go today; and ere I do,*
> *It shall be what o'clock I say it is.'*

The next day, as Petruchio, Kate and Hortensio set out for Baptista's house, Petruchio was still determined to prove that he was Kate's master. He pointed at the sun and remarked how brightly the moon was shining. When Kate argued that it was the sun, he declared that they would turn their horses back unless she agreed with him. Kate had, by this time, realized that there was no point in contradicting her intractable husband and she agreed with whatever he said.

Next, they came across an old gentleman, and Petruchio addressed him as a fair young maid and asked Kate to embrace her. Kate immediately obeyed him, speaking of him as a beautiful young woman. Petruchio changed his tune.

'Why, how now, Kate! I hope thou art not mad:
This is a man, old, wrinkled, faded, wither'd,
And not a maiden, as thou say'st he is.'

Kate instantly changed her impression and apologized to the old man, who was also travelling to Padua. This happened to be Vincentio, the real father of Lucentio, who was going to Baptista's house to meet his son. Petruchio broke the news of Lucentio's wedding to Bianca, who was a noble lady with a wealthy dowry, as they resumed their journey to Padua.

Lucentio and Bianca were in church waiting to be wed by the priest. Vincentio had arrived at Lucentio's house, only to be challenged by the aged scholar who was disguised as Vincentio. After a verbal fight, the scholar denounced Vincentio and asked for him to be taken to jail. At that moment, Baptista, Tranio and the scholar came out of the house and Vincentio recognized Tranio wearing Lucentio's clothing. Overwrought, he asked where his son was.

Happily, at that moment, the newlyweds, Lucentio and Bianca arrived, and Lucentio knelt before his father. As he explained the whole story, the scholar and Tranio disappeared from the scene, unwilling to face the enraged Vincentio. However, Lucentio convinced his father that Tranio had taken his place with his knowledge.

'Love wrought these miracles. Bianca's love
Made me exchange my state with Tranio.'

As they wrangled over the situation, Petruchio and Kate watched in amazement. Kate wanted to follow the proceedings to the end, and Petruchio asked her for a kiss.

When she refused, since it was a public place, Petruchio threatened that they would turn the horses around and go home right away. Kate conceded and gave him a kiss, proving that maybe, love had blossomed between them.

Lucentio threw a grand banquet to celebrate three weddings: those of Petruchio and Katherine, Lucentio and Bianca and Hortensio and his wealthy widow. As the feasting was on, an argument broke out between Kate and the widow, but Bianca calmed them down and the three women left the room.

The other men now teased Petruchio about being stuck with a shrew for a wife. Petruchio offered a wager to the two men to prove whose wife was the most obedient.

> *'Let's each one send unto his wife;*
> *And he whose wife is most obedient*
> *To come at first when he doth send for her,*
> *Shall win the wager which we will propose.'*

The wager was fixed at a hundred crowns. Lucentio was the first one to send for Bianca, confident that she would obey him. The servant returned to say that Bianca said she was busy and could not come. Next was Hortensio's turn and he called for his wife. Prompt came the response. The widow thought that it was a jest and wanted him to go to her instead.

Petruchio laughed at them. He then sent a message through Grumio, commanding Katherine to come to him. The others were certain that Katherine would not come, and they were flabbergasted when she meekly made an appearance.

Petruchio asked her where her sister and the widow were, and she replied that they were conversing by the parlour fire. Petruchio ordered her to go and fetch them at once. Katherine went inside to do his bidding. The men were taken aback and Baptista so impressed that he offered to add twenty thousand crowns to the wager. Petruchio was not done. He offered to show them more instances of his wife's obedience.

When the women returned, Petruchio addressed Katherine, telling her to throw down her cap and stamp on it as it did not suit her. She obeyed him instantly, as the two women looked on, hoping that they would never be brought to such a sorry pass ever. Petruchio then asked Katherine to give a speech to the other two on their duties to their husbands.

Katherine launched into her speech without hesitation. She asked them not to frown upon their husbands who were their lords and masters and who laboured painfully to keep their wives happy and at peace. A woman who was sulky and disobedient was like a graceless traitor to her husband, who only craved love, fair looks and obedience in return. Katherine's speech revealed how much she had changed, as she said,

> *'I am ashamed that women are so simple*
> *To offer war where they should kneel for peace.'*

She ended by admitting that once, she too had been haughty and bad-tempered, but that she had seen the folly of her ways and was now completely obedient to her husband. The wager had been won and Petruchio was richer for it. He and his Kate would live happily together.

All the others were amazed at the change in Katherine, and a victorious Petruchio and she retired for the night, leaving Hortensio and Lucentio still steeped in wonder.

Brief Note

The Taming of the Shrew was written sometime between 1590 and 1592, a comic play in five acts. It was printed in the First Folio of 1623.

It is one of the Bard's comedies, bringing alive the typical shrewish woman who is tamed by the swaggering young man, replete with witty banter and slapstick, frustrated suitors, comic actions, complicated plots and mistaken identities. The audience enjoys the humour of the situation, especially when it hits close to their own lives. It is not a happily-ever-after situation, but instead, one which encompasses the travails that ensue after marriage.

The play also throws light on how matrimony is often a 'matter of money' and explores romantic relationships through a social lens. It explores the Elizabethan norms of gender, and the roles of spouses in marriage. Shakespeare took inspiration from existing folktales about shrewish wives being tamed by aggressive husbands and added his stamp of comedy to his play, poking fun at themes like misogyny, social hierarchy and education.

In short, *The Taming of the Shrew* was a play written mainly to entertain so that the playwright could pay his bills.

3

A MIDSUMMER NIGHT'S DREAM

3.1: *A Midsummer Night's Dream.*
Artist: Vrindha Nair.

Characters in the Order of their Appearance

Theseus, the Duke of Athens
Hippolyta, his fiancée
Egeus, an older nobleman

Hermia, Egeus's daughter
Demetrius, an Athenian youth, in love with Hermia
Lysander, an Athenian youth also in love with Hermia
Helena, an Athenian maiden in love with Demetrius
Peter Quince, a carpenter
Nick Bottom, a talkative weaver
Titania, the Queen of the Fairies
Robin Goodfellow/Puck, Oberon's jester and
a mischievous fairy
Oberon, the King of the Fairies

Theseus, the Duke of Athens and Hippolyta, his fiancée, were in seventh heaven. They were discussing their wedding which was after four days. The Duke wanted the youth of Athens to spend the next few days in merriment so that he himself could wed his lady love in pomp and triumph.

As they were conversing, Egeus, a nobleman, walked in with his daughter, Hermia, and two handsome young Athenians, Lysander and Demetrius. He was upset with his daughter because she had not heeded his words. Egeus wanted her to accept Demetrius as her future husband. Hermia had, unfortunately, fallen in love with Lysander, who had wooed her with bracelets, rings and little trinkets.

The law of Athens was clear on the matter. A daughter had to concede to her father's wishes or be put to death. Egeus pleaded with the Duke to enforce this law on his daughter.

'As she is mine, I may dispose of her:
Which shall be either to this gentleman
Or to her death, according to our law.'

The Duke advised Hermia to listen to her father to whom she owed her birth. Hermia was adamant that Lysander was as worthy a gentleman as Demetrius.

'I would my father look'd but with my eyes.'

She asked the Duke what the worst punishment would be if she disobeyed her father. The Duke answered that the choice was between death and living the life of a nun. Hermia chose the latter, refusing to change her allegiance. The Duke granted her time till his wedding day and asked her to consider her options. She could prepare to die, disobeying her father's will, marry Demetrius or take up the life of a nun.

Demetrius pleaded with Hermia to change her mind. Lysander replied for her.

'You have her father's love, Demetrius;
Let me have Hermia's.'

Lysander was as well born as Demetrius, as wealthy and besides, he was loved by Hermia. He accused Demetrius of having wooed another beautiful maiden, Helena, who was in love with him, whom he had deserted after he met Hermia. Theseus had also heard similar rumours. However, he ordered Hermia to come to a decision soon, and all of them left, leaving Hermia and Lysander alone.

Hermia was pale and unhappy. Lysander assured her saying,

'The course of true love never did run smooth.'

He spoke of a wealthy aunt of his who lived seven leagues away from Athens. Since she was childless, she looked upon Lysander as her own son. Hermia and he could elope and get married at her house, which was outside the limits of Athenian law. Hermia was elated. As they spoke of their plan, Helena entered, sad and frustrated about the fact that Demetrius had eyes only for Hermia. She pleaded with Hermia to teach her to be more like her.

> *'O, teach me how you look, and with what art*
> *You sway the motion of Demetrius' heart.'*

Hermia consoled her saying that she and Lysander were planning to elope. She hoped that Demetrius would turn to Helena after that.

Left alone, Helena lamented over how Demetrius had once loved her. She reasoned that if she told him of Hermia's plan to elope with Lysander, Demetrius would follow them to the woods and she herself would have a chance to win back his love.

> *'I will go tell him of fair Hermia's flight:*
> *Then to the wood will he to-morrow night*
> *Pursue her.'*

Meanwhile, a motley group of workmen were preparing to act out a play for the nuptials of the Duke and Hippolyta. The name of the play was *The Most Lamentable Comedy and Most Cruel Death of Pyramus and Thisbe*. The roles were handed out by Peter Quince, a carpenter, who kept getting interrupted by Nick Bottom, the talkative weaver. The group decided to learn their parts and rehearse in the woods the following night.

Deep in the woods, two fairies met. One was a follower of Queen Titania, the Fairy Queen, and the other was named Robin Goodfellow, known as Puck for short. He was the servant of Oberon, the King of the Fairies. Oberon and Titania had quarrelled over a charming little Indian boy who dwelt with Titania. Oberon had set his heart on acquiring him because he wanted him to be his attendant, but Titania refused to give him up. His late mother had been her devotee and hence, she wanted to keep the boy to honour her memory.

Oberon was incensed. He ordered Puck to go round the world and get him a certain flower which had been shot at with the arrow of Cupid, the God of Love. The milk-white flower had turned into a deep purple, and if its juice was dropped on the eyelid of any man or woman, they would wake up and fall in love with the first creature that came before them.

> *'Fetch me that flower; the herb I shew'd thee once:*
> *The juice of it on sleeping eyelids laid*
> *Will make man or woman madly dote*
> *Upon the next live creature that it sees.'*

The vengeful Oberon wanted to try this on Titania so that she would fall in love with a lion, a bear or monkey.

As Puck vanished, Demetrius walked in, followed by a pleading Helena. Oberon was invisible and he heard what they were saying. Demetrius was clearly upset with Hermia for having eloped with Lysander. He spurned Helena's advances, but she was determined to follow him, despite his hatred. Oberon's heart melted and he vowed that before the two left the woods, he would make Demetrius fall in love with Helena.

> *'Fare thee well, nymph: ere he do leave this grove,*
> *Thou shalt fly him and he shall seek thy love.'*

By then, Puck had returned with the flower. Oberon wanted to streak Titania's eyelids with the juice. Meanwhile, he ordered Puck to look for a young disdainful lad in Athenian clothes and place some juice on his eyelids, so that he would fall in love with the young lady who was following him around. Evidently, he meant Demetrius and Helena.

Titania was lulled to sleep by her fairies, and when they left, Oberon came in quietly and squeezed the juice onto her eyelids. He hoped that she would wake up and fall in love with some vile creature that appeared before her.

Hermia and Lysander had lost their way in the woods. Exhausted, they decided to lie down and rest. Hermia beseeched Lysander to find a bed for himself, some distance away from the grassy bank she had found for herself. As they slept, Puck appeared, having searched for the young Athenian in vain. When he set eyes on Lysander, he mistook him for Demetrius and he quickly dropped the juice on his eyelids.

Demetrius wandered in, followed by Helena. Once again, he scorned her, asking her not to follow him, and moved on. Helena, by then, was out of breath, and she lamented that she was not as beautiful as Hermia. As she caught her breath, she suddenly noticed Lysander asleep on the ground, and wondered if he were dead or alive. She called out to him, and when Lysander opened his eyes, the magic of the juice made him instantly fall in love with Helena. He spoke of his love for her.

'Not Hermia but Helena I love:
Who will not change a raven for a dove?'

Helena was upset because she thought that he was mocking her. She had already been turned down by Demetrius and she felt that Lysander was adding insult to injury by declaring his love for her. She lamented aloud,

'Wherefore was I to this keen mockery born?
When at your hands did I deserve this scorn?'

This time, she moved away, and Lysander glanced at Hermia, whom he loved no more, and went after Helena. A nightmare woke Hermia up and she called out to Lysander to rescue her, but he was long gone.

It was now time for the motley players to rehearse their parts in the forest. They discussed their roles and the various props needed for the play. Puck came across them and was amused at their efforts. Since he was a troublemaker, he replaced the merry Bottom's head with that of an ass. When the others saw him thus, they were petrified and ran away. Bottom wondered why they had deserted him but decided to sing to prove that he was not afraid of being alone in the forest.

3.2: *A Midsummer Night's Dream.*
Artist: Krishna N.P.

Bottom's song woke Titania up and she called out,

'What angel wakes me from my flowery bed?'

The magic juice had done its trick again. Titania fell in love with the clumsy weaver with the head of an ass. She summoned her fairies and asked them to tend to him and take care of his every need. Puck gave Oberon an account of how he had beguiled the players and of how Titania had fallen in love with Bottom.

'Titania waked and straightaway loved an ass.'

Puck went on to tell him about how he had dropped the juice on the eyelids of an Athenian. However, when Demetrius and Hermia walked in a little while later, Oberon realized that Puck had applied the juice on the wrong man. This time, Demetrius was pleading with Hermia, but to no avail. Hermia accused him of having murdered Lysander for she knew that he would never have left her alone willingly. Demetrius denied that he had harmed Lysander, but Hermia was not willing to hear anything more.

A dejected Demetrius decided to rest for a while. He lay down and went to sleep. Oberon rebuked Puck for having applied the juice on the wrong man's eyelids. He told him to search for the lovesick Helena and bring her to the spot where Demetrius lay asleep so that they could amend the mistake. Next, Oberon placed a little juice on the sleeping man's eyelids.

Puck came back soon. Helena and Lysander were at hand, with the latter declaring his love for Helena. Oberon and Puck stood away to watch the confusion that ensued.

As Lysander wooed Helena, swearing that he did not love Hermia anymore, Demetrius suddenly awoke. His eyes fell on Helena and he fell in love with her in an instant. He proclaimed,

'O Helena, goddess, nymph, perfect, divine!'

Helena was almost in tears. She thought that both the men were mocking her. When Lysander told Demetrius that he could have Hermia, he retorted,

'Lysander, keep thy Hermia; I will none:
If e'er I loved her, all that love is gone.'

At that juncture, Hermia wandered in, having heard Lysander's loved voice and she asked him why he had left her alone. She was aghast to hear Lysander talking of his love for Helena. The tables had, indeed, turned. Earlier both men had been in love with Hermia, and now both spoke of their adoration for Helena. Helena believed that Hermia too was part of the plot against her. Fierce words were exchanged between them all, and Hermia was furious when Helena referred to her lack of height and called her a vixen.

'And though she be little, she is fierce.'

Finally, the two young men decided to have a duel to sort out the matter. Helena was afraid that Hermia would harm her and she too left after them. Oberon berated Puck and ordered him to set things right. He directed him to create a fog and confuse the two men by calling out to them in the other's voice. Puck did just that and he led them both a merry dance, till, exhausted and bemused, they fell asleep.

By then, both Helena and Hermia had also wandered to the same spot, and they too lay down and fell asleep. Puck then applied another herb on Lysander's eyes, one which would counter the effects of the love juice.

'When thou wakest,
Thou takest
True delight
In the sight
Of thy former lady's eye.'

Once that was done, Puck stole away. When the four woke the next morning, everything would appear to be a midsummer night's dream. Meanwhile, Oberon had managed to persuade Titania to part with the little boy, and once the boy was his, he undid the magic that had forced her to fall in love with Bottom. When Titania awoke, she was sheepish about the whole episode. As they heard the morning lark, they moved away while Puck restored the oblivious Bottom to his former self.

At dawn, Theseus, along with Hippolyta and Egeus, walked into the glade, only to find the young lovers asleep. They were surprised to see how they, who had been bitter rivals, now slept peacefully at the same spot. Theseus questioned Lysander and Demetrius.

'I know you two are rival enemies;
How comes this gentle concord in the world?'

Lysander replied that he had no idea about what had happened, and that he and Hermia had stolen away from Athens to be together. Egeus was furious and requested the Duke to punish them because they had deceived both him and Demetrius. Demetrius explained that he had followed the two to seek Hermia's love and Helena had followed him. However, by some power above, his love for Hermia had melted away only to be replaced by his love for Helena.

> *'The object and pleasure of mine eye*
> *Is only Helena.'*

The Duke was pleased. He proclaimed that both the couples would be wed along with him and Hippolyta at the Athenian temple, followed by a great and solemn feast.

> *'Egeus, I will overbear your will;*
> *For in the temple by and by with us*
> *These couples shall eternally be knit.'*

There was mayhem at Peter Quince's house for Bottom had not returned from the woods and their play could not be staged without him. They were downcast because it would have been a matter of prestige and money to have performed at the Duke's nuptials. Suddenly, to their immense joy, Bottom came in and urged them to hurry and get their costumes ready as the Duke and his new bride were eager to witness their play.

The actors came forth and played their parts, much to the amusement of the audience, who joked about the various characters. The play ended and was followed by a dance, after which they all retired for the night. Oberon and Titania appeared with their fairies to bless the couples with true love and happiness, and their unborn children with beauty. No harm would ever come to the owner of the palace, Theseus and his wife, Hippolyta.

It was left to Puck to have the last word, and he prepared to make amends for all the mischief he had wrought. He ended by proclaiming,

'If we shadows have offended,
Think but this, and all is mended,
That you have but slumber'd here,
While these visions did appear.'

Brief Note

A Midsummer Night's Dream is one of the best-loved plays of Shakespeare, written in 1595. It was written around the same time as *Romeo and Juliet*. The play within the play, *Pyramus and Thisbe* has close parallels with *Romeo and Juliet* with comic undertones.

A Midsummer Night's Dream reveals a world of opposites— the conflict between love and social conventions, as also the conflict between fantasy and reality. It is highly entertaining, interspersed as it is with music and dance, allied with magic and merriment and mayhem.

Back in time, the grand spectacle, populated with fairies and humans, entranced the Elizabethan audience. It was even believed that the play was performed at an aristocratic wedding where Queen Elizabeth I was herself present. While the play spoke of the power of love, it also revealed the follies of lovers, and the benevolence of Nature that protected all the characters who wandered around in the mist, deep in the forest of Athens.

Thus, it is no wonder that this play is one of the most fascinating of Shakespeare's plays, replete with stage effects and costumes, melodrama and mischief. It gets so fantastical that at the end, Demetrius asks in wonder after he awakes from a deep sleep.

'Are you sure/That we are awake?

It seems to me? That yet we sleep, we dream.'

Act 4, Scene 1

4

THE MERCHANT OF VENICE

4.1: *The Merchant of Venice.*
Artist: Aditya Sujith.

Characters in the Order of their Appearance

Antonio, the Merchant of Venice
Salarino, Antonio's friend
Bassanio, Antonio's closest friend

Lorenzo, Jessica's husband
Gratiano, Bassanio's man servant
Portia/Balthazar, Bassanio's lady love
Nerissa/Young Clerk, Portia's woman servant
The Prince of Morocco
The Prince of Arragon
Jessica, Shylock's daughter
Messenger
Shylock, a Jewish moneylender
The Duke of Venice

In Venice, there once lived a merchant named Antonio. He had many ships laden with cargo travelling the perilous seas. One day, his friends found him downcast. They asked him about his ships, trying to cheer him up in various ways. Antonio assured them that his business was fine, mainly because he had not tied up all his ventures in one place, nor placed all his eggs in one basket.

'Why, then you are in love,' said Salarino, half-mockingly.

Antonio denied that he was in love.

The conversation was interrupted by the arrival of three gentlemen—Bassanio, Lorenzo and Gratiano. Gratiano was perturbed at how unwell Antonio looked and pointed out that he was 'marvellously changed'. His reply was,

> *'I hold the world but as the world, Gratiano;*
> *A stage where every man must play a part,*
> *And mine a sad one.'*

Antonio and Bassanio were extremely close friends. Bassanio had often borrowed large sums of money from Antonio, and he was now prepared to borrow more because he had fallen in love.

Antonio was all ears. He wanted to hear about Bassanio's lady love, Portia, a wealthy heiress who lived in Belmont.

'Well, tell me now what lady is the same
To whom you swore a secret pilgrimage,
That you to-day promised to tell me of?'

Bassanio was only too ready to speak about his Portia who was beautiful and accomplished. Hence, renowned suitors from across the globe were vying to marry her. Bassanio wanted to woo her and once again, he needed Antonio to help him financially.

Antonio assured Bassanio that he would do whatever was needed to get him his lady love. Bassanio replied in gratitude,

'To you, Antonio, I owe the most, in money and in love.'

Meanwhile, in Belmont, the beautiful Portia was unhappy. Her late father, who had been concerned about her finding a suitable husband, had devised a kind of a lottery through which she would find the right man, or so he had believed. She had no such hope, and she grumbled to her maid, Nerissa, about her father's will.

'I may
neither choose whom I would nor refuse whom I
dislike; so is the will of a living daughter curbed
by the will of a dead father.'

There were three caskets of gold, silver and lead respectively, and in one of them nestled a photograph of Portia. The suitors who thronged for her hand would have to pick the one with the photograph. If they failed, they would have to vow never to marry in their lives.

This threat had frightened away many suitors, all of whom Portia had dismissed for their many eccentricities. Nerissa was regaling her mistress with the names of these unfortunate suitors, while Portia poked fun at them.

The suitors had diverse personalities. For example, the Neapolitan Prince spoke only of his horse, and had no other conversation. The Palatine count had a constant frown, and the French lord had a colourless personality. There was an Englishman who knew no language except English while Portia knew hardly any. The German suitor suffered from the malady of drunkenness.

Nerissa then introduced a name that intrigued Portia, that of a young Venetian, a scholar and a soldier, Bassanio.

'True, madam: he, of all the men that ever my foolish eyes looked upon, was the best deserving a fair lady.'

As they were thus conversing, there came news about the arrival that night of a new suitor, the Prince of Morocco. Portia sighed. If only she could get rid of this new wooer as easily as the others! However, she had to welcome him with a good grace.

The Prince of Morocco fortified himself to make his choice of the caskets. He looked at the three, carefully reading the inscriptions on each. The shining gold casket attracted his attention. The inscription read,

'Who chooseth me shall gain what many men desire.'

The silver one came next and its inscription read,

'Who chooseth me shall get as much as he deserves.'

The final one was a dull leaden one. The Prince bent over it and read,

'Who chooseth me must give and hazard all he hath.'

The Prince finally chose the golden casket. He unlocked it only to find a death's head with a scroll in its eye socket, which proclaimed that all that glitters is not gold. He left, too grieved for a lengthy farewell, much to Portia's relief.

The next suitor was the Prince of Arragon. He strode in, casting an arrogant eye over the caskets. He mocked at those who made choices with the majority, and finally settled on the silver casket because he could not imagine that dull lead could contain Portia's picture. When he opened it, he paused, obviously upset. Inside was the picture of a fool's head with a schedule along with it, which mentioned that whoever chose silver would get what he deserved. The Prince remarked wryly that he had come with one fool's head and was going back with two. He quickly made his exit as well.

While Portia was discussing her latest suitors with Nerissa, Bassanio decided to make his way to Belmont to take his chance with the fair lady. He invited Gratiano, his boisterous man servant, to accompany him, warning him that he had to tone down his wild and loud behaviour and be more restrained. Or else Bassanio would lose his chance with Portia, given his companion's boorish nature. Gratiano assured him that he would be solemn and modest and watch his manners as if trying to please his own grandmother.

When they reached Belmont, Bassanio was eager to try his luck to win Portia's hand. Portia wanted to delay him because she feared that he would have to leave her if he failed. She longed to help him make the right choice, but she was bound by her oath to her father. She was bewitched by Bassanio's eyes which had divided her into two. She claimed that both parts of her belonged to him, and yet, till he made the right choice, she could not, in reality, belong to him.

'One half of me is yours, the other half yours,
Mine own, I would say; but if mine, then yours,
And so all yours.'

Bassanio pored over the three caskets, convinced that appearances could be deceptive. He spurned the gaudy gold one and the pale, common silver one, making humble lead his choice, despite the warning that whoever chose lead would have to give and risk everything he had. When he found her picture within, he was elated, for he had won his fair lady. He could not believe his good fortune until Portia assured him,

'Myself and what is mine to you and yours
Is now converted.'

Along with her beautiful mansion and her household of servants, she presented him with a ring, warning him that he would lose her love if he parted with or lost the ring. He responded saying that the day he took off the ring would be his last day on earth.

Gratiano, in the meantime, had fallen in love with Nerissa, and had won her heart. He said to Bassanio,

'You saw the mistress, I beheld the maid. You loved,
I loved.'

A messenger from Venice arrived at that moment. He handed Bassanio a letter from Antonio. A heartbroken Bassanio explained to Portia how he had borrowed money from his dear friend Antonio who had lost his ships at sea, every one of them. Bassanio read the letter out.

> *'Sweet Bassanio, my ships have all miscarried, my creditors grow cruel, my estate is very low, my bond to the Jew is forfeit; and since in paying it, it is impossible I should live, all debts are cleared between you and I, if I might but see you at my death.'*

A miserly Jew, Shylock, had apparently sworn that he would have a pound of Antonio's flesh rather than twenty times the same sum of money. He was a much-despised moneylender. He lent money at exorbitant rates and hated Antonio for many reasons, one of the primary ones being his practice of lending money minus interest. Antonio too abhorred the sight of the Jew. He scorned him and considered him an enemy.

Bassanio, who was in desperate need of money to woo Portia, had spoken to Shylock and asked him for three thousand ducats, to be repaid over three months. Antonio had agreed to stand guarantee for the loan.

A long-standing, fierce hatred raged in Shylock's heart against Antonio. Antonio had called him names in public, spat into his beard and kicked him like a dog. Even at a time like this, Antonio told Shylock to lend him the money as to an enemy and not a friend, so that he could take the penalty with a better face.

That was when Shylock threw a bombshell. He said that he would provide three thousand ducats, and if the money was not returned in three months, he expected a pound of flesh from any part of Antonio's body.

'If you repay me not on such a day,
In such a place, such sum or sums as are
Express'd in the condition, let the forfeit
Be nominated for an equal pound
Of your fair flesh, to be cut off and taken
In what part of your body pleaseth me.'

Antonio agreed because he was confident that he would get three times the value of the bond within a couple of months. Bassanio was not as confident, because he mistrusted the Jew. Shylock told them to get the bond drawn up by a notary while he would go home and get the money.

And now, Antonio was on the brink of being bankrupt as all his ships had been lost at sea.

Having heard the whole story, Portia urged Bassanio to marry her first and then leave for Venice. She offered him enough money to pay off Antonio's debt twenty times over. After Bassanio left, Portia devised a plan where she and Nerissa would make their way to Venice, disguised as men, so that their brand-new husbands would see them, but not recognize them. She said to Nerissa jokingly,

'When we are both accoutred like young men,
I'll prove the prettier fellow of the two.'

Shylock's daughter, Jessica, was ashamed of being his daughter, mainly because he was a Jew. She did feel guilty because he was not a hard-hearted father. She was in love with Lorenzo, a Christian, and the plan was that she would dress up like a boy and pretend to be Lorenzo's torchbearer. She would elope with him and carry her gold and jewels as well. Shylock was invited for supper with Bassanio, and he instructed Jessica to lock the doors and remain within. Little did he suspect that she would leave the house before he returned, though he did have a premonition of something ill brewing. After Shylock left for supper, Jessica said to herself,

'Farewell; and if my fortune be not crost,
I have a father, you a daughter, lost.'

Soon after, Lorenzo arrived with his friends and Jessica abandoned her home, and her father, to make a new life for herself with her sweetheart. When Shylock returned, he was extremely upset that his daughter had eloped, and even more so that she had taken his money and his precious jewels.

However, Shylock also had reason to rejoice. Antonio's ship, laden with expensive cargo, had been wrecked at sea, leading to a massive loss in his business. Shylock gloated over the loss, and when Salarino, a friend of Antonio's, questioned him about his pound of flesh agreement, he replied that it would feed his revenge. He was livid at Antonio's insults over the years, insults hurled against him all because he was a usurer and a Jew.

'Hath not a Jew eyes? Hath not a Jew hands, organs,
dimensions senses, affections, passions?'

Shylock continued ranting against Antonio. He had obviously been badly hurt by him.

'If you prick us, do we not bleed? If you tickle us, do we
not laugh? If you poison us, do we not die? And if you
wrong us, shall we not revenge?'

While Shylock rejoiced at Antonio's losses at sea, he lamented that there was no news of his daughter, Jessica, except that she was squandering her jewels on creditors.

However, he looked forward to taking revenge on his arch-rival, Antonio, at the court.

At the Venetian court, the Duke himself tried to persuade Shylock to drop his insistence on the pound of flesh. Bassanio offered the hard-hearted Jew six thousand ducats instead of three. Shylock stuck to his guns, refusing to see reason.

4.2: *The Merchant of Venice.*
Artist: Manasa Kalyan.

Meanwhile, the Duke had despatched a message to a legal expert who sent a young and skilful lawyer, Balthazar, who was apparently familiar with the case of Antonio versus Shylock. When Portia walked in, disguised as Balthazar, accompanied by Nerissa in the guise of her male clerk, the Duke welcomed her. Portia addressed Shylock and requested him to be merciful. Shylock asked her why he should show mercy. Portia's reply was classic.

'The quality of mercy is not strained.
It droppeth as the gentle rain from heaven
Upon the place beneath.'

Portia's plea was that mercy was far above the earthly power that kings enjoyed and was an attribute of God himself. She requested Shylock to show mercy towards Antonio. Shylock was not in the least swayed by her persuasion. Bassanio pleaded with the Duke to bend the law. Portia denied him that request saying that there was no law in Venice that could change an established decree. Elated to hear this, Shylock exclaimed,

'A Daniel come to judgment, yea, a Daniel! —
O wise young judge, how I do honour thee!'

Portia then read the bond which offered the Jew thrice the amount of money. Shylock insisted that he had made an oath and would not perjure his soul by denying it. Portia then proclaimed to the court that since Antonio had not paid Shylock the money, the latter could lawfully claim a pound of flesh nearest Antonio's heart. Once again, she entreated Shylock to be merciful.

'Why, this bond is forfeit;
And lawfully by this the Jew may claim
A pound of flesh, to be by him cut off
Nearest the merchant's heart. Be merciful:
Take thrice thy money; bid me tear the bond.'

Shylock repeated that he would stick to the contract since nobody would be able to force him to change his mind.

> *'I crave the law,*
> *The penalty and forfeit of my bond.'*

The tension in the court was heightened as Portia requested Antonio to bare his chest for the knife. Shylock praised the young lawyer for his wisdom and fairness. Portia asked him if the scales were ready to measure the pound of flesh and he said they were. When she checked whether he had arranged the services of a surgeon to stop Antonio from bleeding to death, Shylock replied that it was not in the contract.

Finally, Antonio bade Bassanio farewell, speaking of his love for him. He asked him to pay his respects to his new bride. Bassanio was so overcome that he replied that dear as his wife was, he would give her up along with life itself and the whole world if he could save Antonio. At this, Portia murmured that his wife would not be happy to hear him say this.

The stage was set for Shylock to cut off his pound of flesh. He moved forward with the knife, and just as he was about to start, Portia stopped him. She said that the bond specified the cutting of exactly one pound of flesh but did not speak about any blood being shed. So, Shylock would have to cut Antonio's flesh without shedding a drop of blood, or else his lands and property would be confiscated by the state of Venice.

Taken aback, Shylock offered to take thrice the money and forfeit the bond. Bassanio was about to give him the money when Portia forestalled him, saying that the

Jew would have more justice than he deserved. She told him clearly that he could cut the pound of flesh with no blood shed, and if the scales turned even by a whisker, signifying that the pound was not exactly one pound, he would be put to death and his property seized.

> *'Take then thy bond, take thou thy pound of flesh,*
> *But in the cutting it if thou dost shed*
> *One drop of Christian blood, thy lands and goods*
> *Are by the laws of Venice confiscate*
> *Unto the state of Venice.'*

Shylock was flabbergasted. Things were not going his way at all. Pushed into a corner, he asked Portia if he could at least get his three thousand ducats back. However, Portia dealt him a final blow. She quoted the Venetian law, where a foreigner who, directly or indirectly, attempted to kill a citizen, had to hand over half his possessions to the wronged person. The other half would go to the state. Only the Duke could grant him mercy.

Shylock was now at his tether's end. The Duke took the opportunity to show him the difference between them by granting him his life. However, Shylock's wealth would be divided between Antonio and the state. Shylock appealed to the Duke to take his life as well since he would be left with nothing to sustain himself.

At that pronouncement, Antonio revealed his magnanimity. He wanted nothing for himself. If the state were willing to set aside the fine for half the property, he would request Shylock to give the other half to Lorenzo, the man who had stolen away his daughter.

Antonio put forth two more conditions. First, Shylock would have to become a Christian and second, he would have to make a gift deed, bequeathing all his property to his daughter and son-in-law after his death. Shylock had no other recourse but to agree. Portia ordered her clerk, the disguised Nerissa, to draw up the deed of the gift. Shylock excused himself from the court, citing ill health and left after having promised to sign the deed.

Bassanio and Antonio were overcome with gratitude. Bassanio offered the three thousand ducats that they owed Shylock to Portia who refused to take it saying that she was satisfied that her job had been done well. Bassanio insisted that she take some memento from them both as a token of their gratitude.

Portia had not forgiven Bassanio for his earlier statement about giving her up. She asked Antonio for his gloves, and then pointed to the ring Bassanio wore. Bassanio was reluctant to give her the ring and finally told her that it was a ring given to him by his wife who had forbidden him from taking it off his finger. He said rather sheepishly,

> *'Good sir, this ring was given me by my wife;*
> *And when she put it on, she made me vow*
> *That I should neither sell nor give nor lose it.'*

Portia waved away his excuses and left with Nerissa. Antonio entreated Bassanio to give the young lawyer the ring because he had earned it with his cleverness, and for their own deep friendship. Bassanio gave in and sent Gratiano with the ring after Portia.

When Gratiano caught up with Portia, he handed over the ring and invited her to dinner with his master. Portia accepted the ring but refused his invitation. She requested him to escort the disguised Nerissa to Shylock's house.

Nerissa, in an aside, told Portia that she too would try and get the ring she had given Gratiano off his finger.

Meanwhile, Lorenzo and Jessica had reached Belmont and were presiding over Portia's mansion. They had arranged musicians to welcome her home. Bassanio was also expected back soon. When Portia walked into her hall, she saw the light shining and said,

'How far that little candle throws his beams!
So shines a good deed in a naughty world.'

Sometime later, Bassanio, Antonio and Gratiano arrived and Bassanio introduced his dear friend to his wife. Portia welcomed them in. Suddenly, she heard Nerissa and Gratiano arguing. The reason was the ring that Gratiano swore he had given to the lawyer's clerk. Gratiano kept swearing that he had given it to a young boy, but Nerissa refused to believe him. Portia agreed with Nerissa. She told Gratiano that he should never have given away his wife's first gift so thoughtlessly. She said that Bassanio would never give away her ring for all the money in the world.

Bassanio had to confess that he had given his ring away to the lawyer who had argued so brilliantly and saved Antonio from death. Portia and Nerissa accused their husbands of having given the rings away to other women. They refused to listen to any more explanations.

It was then that Antonio stepped forward stating the whole quarrel was about him. He tried to explain matters when Portia handed him the ring, asking him to advise Bassanio to keep it more safely than the earlier one. She revealed that it was she who had disguised herself as the lawyer, Balthazar, and Nerissa her clerk. She also handed over a letter to Antonio with the good news that three of his ships had arrived at the harbour, loaded with wealth.

Nerissa presented the deed that Shylock had signed to Lorenzo, which testified that, after the death of the Jew, all his possessions would come to him and Jessica.

It was time for questions to be asked and answers given, and for the loose ends to be tied up. Gratiano's parting shot was an amusing one:

> *'Well, while I live I'll fear no other thing*
> *So sore as keeping safe Nerissa's ring.'*

Brief Note

The Merchant of Venice was written in 1596–1597 and ranks as one of the most frequently performed plays of William Shakespeare. While Antonio is the merchant of Venice mentioned in the title, his role is overshadowed by that of Shylock, the Jewish moneylender, a character who is reviled in the play for his grasping nature. However, many are the arguments in favour of Shylock, and for the harsh treatment against him by Antonio and many others. There are several references to the mistrust and the hatred between the Christians and the Jews in the play that reflect the prejudices that existed in Elizabethan times.

Portia plays a significant role, proving herself cleverer than the male characters. In fact, all the three female characters in the play are strong women—Portia, Nerissa and Jessica, a fact that was ironic at a time when women were not considered equal to men.

The play has thrown up certain phrases that have stayed on in the hearts and minds of people. 'A pound of flesh' and 'with bated breath' are two examples. Portia's speech beginning with 'The quality of mercy' and Shylock's rant 'Hath not a Jew eyes?' come to the lips the moment the play is mentioned. The original quote—'all that glisters is not gold' in the 1596 edition of the play was later replaced by the more common 'all that glitters is not gold' in later editions.

On 10th February, 1605, the play was performed before King James I, who enjoyed it so much that he asked for an encore performance in the following week.

5

JULIUS CAESAR

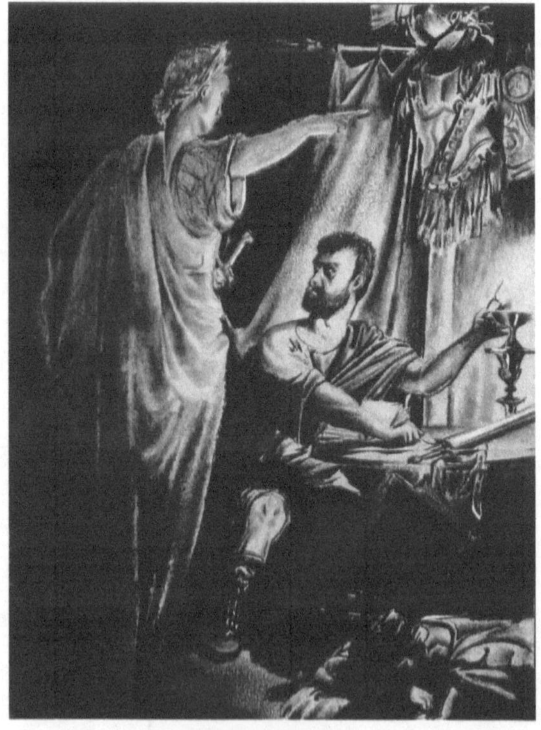

5.1: *Julius Caesar.*
Artist: Pranav Prakash.

Characters in the Order of their Appearance

Julius Caesar, the great Roman Emperor
Calpurnia, Caesar's wife
Mark Antony, Caesar's closest friend

**Marcus Brutus, a prominent Roman senator and
unwilling conspirator
Gaius Cassius, a Roman senator and conspirator
Casca, a Roman senator and conspirator
Soothsayer
Decius Brutus, a Roman senator and conspirator
Octavius Caesar, Caesar's grandnephew and adopted son
Portia, Brutus's wife**

The great Roman general, Julius Caesar, had defeated his rival, Pompey, in the Battle of Pharsalus and returned triumphantly to Rome. The elated commoners in Rome were waiting to celebrate his victory. As Caesar strode through the streets, along with his wife Calpurnia, his friend, Mark Antony and other prominent Romans like Brutus, Cassius and Casca, he was suddenly stopped by a voice in the crowd.

*'Who is it in the press that calls on me?
I hear a tongue, shriller than all the music,
Cry "Caesar!" Speak; Caesar is turn'd to hear.'*

It was a soothsayer who had a cryptic warning for him.

'Beware the ides of March.'

The ides referred to the fifteenth day of March. Even though the man repeated his warning twice, Caesar did not heed it and turned away. Two fellow Romans, Brutus and Cassius, moved away to have a conversation. Cassius had a plot in his mind, and he wanted to seek out Brutus' opinion about Caesar. Brutus, of late, had conflicting thoughts and Cassius convinced him that Brutus and Caesar were both equally respected in Rome. He himself did not want to bow down before a person whom he did not consider his superior. He referred to Caesar as a Colossus.

> *'Why, man, he doth bestride the narrow world*
> *Like a Colossus, and we petty men*
> *Walk under his huge legs and peep about*
> *To find ourselves dishonourable graves.'*

Cassius' words were convincing. His frustration revealed itself as he said,

> *'The fault, dear Brutus, is not in our stars,*
> *But in ourselves, that we are underlings.'*

Meanwhile, Caesar, who had returned with his train of people, was looking troubled. Casca, who had been with him, stayed behind to inform Cassius and Brutus that Antony had offered Caesar the crown of Rome thrice, and all three times Caesar had refused it. He had fainted before the crowd, which displayed its loyalty by cheering for him.

Amid a fearful storm, Cassius and Casca discussed how the Roman senators had decided to crown Caesar at the Capitol the next morning. Cassius had already spoken to some of the noblest-minded Romans and they had agreed to be part of a dangerous conspiracy to assassinate Caesar. Brutus was the only one who needed to be convinced to be part of this conspiracy, but Cassius was confident that he too would join them in their enterprise. Hence, after midnight, the conspirators made their way to Brutus' house, where he had already received a paper asking him to speak, strike and redress, a note against Caesar planted there by the conspirators.

The conspirators planned to assassinate Caesar, but Brutus warned them their deed should appear as a purge of the state, and not murder. He disapproved of their harming Mark Antony, Caesar's closest friend, because he felt that once Caesar was no more, Antony would lose his strength.

> *'We shall be call'd purgers, not murderers.*
> *And for Mark Antony, think not of him;*
> *For he can do no more than Caesar's arm*
> *When Caesar's head is off.'*

Before the conspirators left, they decided that Decius Brutus, one of them, would escort Caesar to the Capitol the next day.

The night was a stormy one, with ill omens being witnessed by many. Caesar himself was disturbed by his wife, Calpurnia, crying out thrice in her sleep,

> *'Help, ho! They murder Caesar!'*

Calpurnia was so horrified by the omens that she pleaded with Caesar not to go out of the house that day. When Caesar refused to listen to her, she said,

> *'When beggars die, there are no comets seen,*
> *The heavens themselves blaze forth the death of princes.'*

However, these words had no effect on Caesar who prided himself on being a courageous man. He replied to his wife,

> *'Cowards die many times before their death;*
> *The valiant never taste of death but once.'*

Calpurnia had finally managed to persuade Caesar not to go to the senate house when Decius Brutus appeared. Caesar told him that he would not be stirring out that day because Calpurnia had dreamt that Caesar's statue was spouting blood like a fountain in which many smiling Romans were washing their hands. She took this as a grave omen.

When Decius heard this, he turned the interpretation of the dream around. He explained that it meant that the Romans would receive life blood from Caesar because they revered him.

> *'It was a vision fair and fortunate:*
> *Your statue spouting blood in many pipes,*
> *In which so many smiling Romans bathed,*
> *Signifies that from you great Rome shall suck*
> *Reviving blood.'*

He mentioned that the Romans had decided to give Caesar a crown. They could well change their minds if he sent word that he would not appear only because his wife had had a bad dream. When Caesar heard this, his mind wavered again, and he decided to go along with Decius Brutus. Meanwhile, all the other Romans came to escort him to the senate house.

At the senate house, Caesar spurned the case of a certain Roman whom he had banished, proclaiming that he could not be won over by sweet words and flattery.

> *'But I am constant as the northern star,*
> *Of whose true-fix'd and resting quality*
> *There is no fellow in the firmament.'*

The fatal moment had arrived. The conspirators surrounded Caesar and stabbed him, one by one. Brutus was the last one of them all, and when Caesar saw him, he was heartbroken. As he fell, his last words were,

> *'Et tu, Brute? Then fall, Caesar!' (You too, Brutus?)*

As the horrifying news of Caesar's assassination spread, Brutus asked the conspirators to wash their hands in his blood and walk through the marketplace, proclaiming 'Peace, Freedom and Liberty'.

Mark Antony, Caesar's dearest friend, had been led away before the assassination. He now sent a servant to Brutus asking him if he could appear before him without any danger to his life. Brutus agreed, relieved that Antony had taken things so well. However, the shrewd Cassius had an inkling that Antony was a danger to them.

Antony was shattered when he saw Caesar lying there, but he masked his true feelings and instead, shook hands with all the conspirators. When Brutus assured him that they had no enmity towards him, Antony requested them to allow him to take Caesar's body to the marketplace and speak as a friend at his funeral. Brutus agreed to his request, but at Cassius's discomfort, warned Antony that he could not denounce the conspirators for Caesar's death. He, Brutus, would speak at the pulpit first and Antony would speak after.

> *'Mark Antony, here, take you Caesar's body.*
> *You shall not in your funeral speech blame us,*
> *But speak all good you can devise of Caesar,*
> *And say you do't by our permission.'*

When Antony was left alone with Caesar's body, he revealed his sorrow and anger at the death of his friend. He was determined to avenge the heinous deed. At Caesar's funeral, he would provoke the Romans to take revenge on the conspirators.

Brutus and Cassius had decided to speak at two different avenues to convince the Romans of their reasons for the assassination. Brutus began his speech by asking the people of Rome to judge whether he had done anything wrong. As an explanation to why he slew Caesar, he said,

'Not that I loved Caesar less, but that I loved Rome more.'

The crowd believed that he had assassinated Caesar to grant them their freedom. As he spoke, Mark Antony came there with Caesar's body and Brutus handed the stage over to him and left the scene. By now, the crowd was convinced that Caesar had been a tyrant and were willing to hear no ill of Brutus.

Mark Antony was a master orator, and he began by saying that he had come to bury Caesar and not to praise him.

'Friends, Romans, countrymen, lend me your ears;
I come to bury Caesar, not to praise him.
The evil that men do lives after them;
The good is oft interred with their bones;
So let it be with Caesar.'

He spoke of how Caesar had thrice refused the crown that the Romans had offered him and about Caesar having wept when the poor cried. He reminded them of how his conquests had filled the coffers of Rome. He slyly kept repeating that Brutus and the others were all honourable men who insisted that Caesar was ambitious. By the middle of his speech, he had undone the effect of Brutus' speech earlier, especially when he cried,

'O judgment! Thou are fled to brutish beasts,
And men have lost their reason.'

Antony then made mention of Caesar's will to whet the mob's appetite further. He diverted their attention towards his wounds, especially mentioning how Brutus, Caesar's angel, had taken him unawares when he stabbed him.

'This was the most unkindest cut of all.'

Antony proclaimed that when Caesar saw Brutus betray him, his mighty heart burst, and he fell at the base of Pompey's statue. At this juncture, Antony dramatically cried out,

'O what a fall was there, my countrymen!
Then I, and you, and all of us fell down,
Whilst bloody treason flourish'd over us.'

As Mark Antony spoke about Caesar's love for his people, the crowd started getting agitated, shouting for revenge. The final straw came when Antony read out Caesar's will in which he had left seventy-five drachmas to every citizen. He had also opened out his magnificent gardens for public use. By now, the mob was inflamed, and they left with Caesar's body, vowing to burn down the houses of the conspirators.

Octavius Caesar, Caesar's heir, had reached Rome by then. Antony went to meet him to discuss how best the will of Caesar be carried out, and how the traitors would meet their deaths.

Meanwhile, Brutus and Cassius who had mustered up their own camps near Philippi to fight against Antony and Octavius, were at loggerheads. Brutus called Cassius corrupt, and accused him of having withheld gold that was to be paid to Brutus' men. Their tempers flared, and then died down only when Brutus told Cassius that his wife, Portia, was no more.

Just then, a messenger came to inform them that Octavius and Antony were on their way to Philippi with a huge army against them. Brutus convinced Cassius to lead their combined army to Philippi so that they could ward the enemy off. Soon Brutus was alone, and as he listened to some light music, an apparition suddenly startled him in the dead of the night. It was the ghost of Julius Caesar who spoke to him and warned him that they would meet on the battlefield of Philippi. A deeply shaken Brutus could not sleep a wink that night.

The next day, the generals of the two armies met and spoke, after which they went back to prepare for war. Brutus and Cassius had a moment together when they spoke of the outcome of the battle that would decide their fates and end the work the ides of March had begun. It was time for them to bid each other an everlasting farewell. Brutus turned to Cassius, saying,

> *'For ever, and for ever, farewell, Cassius!*
> *If we do meet again, why, we shall smile;*
> *If not, why then, this parting was well made.'*

Cassius replied in a similar vein and they parted ways. Sadly, that was their final parting as Cassius stabbed himself over a misunderstanding, leaving Brutus to mourn for him. The battle was one-sided and soon, Brutus' army was routed. Brutus knew that his end was near as he had witnessed the ghost of Caesar twice. He preferred death to being taken captive and he died, running into his own sword.

The battle was over and when Antony and Octavius arrived, flushed with victory, they found that Brutus was no more. Antony praised Brutus, calling him the noblest Roman of them all since he had been part of the conspiracy against Caesar only for the greater good of Rome. He ordered that Brutus would be accorded all respect and rites of burial, as an honoured soldier deserved. He ended by saying,

> *'His life was gentle, and the elements*
> *So mix'd in him that Nature might stand up*
> *And say to all the world, "This was a man!"'*

Brief Note

Julius Caesar is one of the most discussed historical plays by William Shakespeare. Written in 1599, it was one of the first of his plays to be performed at the Globe Theatre. The Bard took an event that influenced the history of Rome and created a powerful play out of it. When one speaks of Julius Caesar, it is the Shakespearean version that first comes to mind.

The play begins with a reference to Roman history when Caesar, who had earlier formed the Triumvirate with two other ambitious men, Pompey and Crassus, found himself at a crossroads. Crassus had died and Pompey had declared Caesar a traitor. Hence, Caesar crossed the Rubicon river into Italy. After initial reverses, he later defeated Pompey and returned triumphant to Rome.

This is a play of action and consequences. The first half of the play leads to the assassination of Caesar, and the second half deals with the consequences of this grave act. Though Caesar is the protagonist in the play, he is overshadowed by Marcus Brutus, who has more dialogues than Caesar, and comes across as a loyal patriot who confesses, 'Not that I loved Caesar less, but that I loved Rome more.'

Mark Antony's speech is considered one of the finest monologues ever in English literature and proves the true power of words as he cleverly manipulates the mob against the conspirators. However, in the end, once again, it is Brutus who receives the accolades from Antony.

'His life was gentle and the elements

So mix'd in him that nature might stand up

And say to all the world, "This was a man."'

6

AS YOU LIKE IT

6.1: *As You Like It.*
Artist: Pavithra S. Nair.

Characters in the Order of their Appearance

Oliver, the eldest son of Sir Rowland de Bois
Orlando, the youngest son of Sir Rowland de Bois
Jacques, the middle son of Sir Rowland de Bois
Adam, a loyal old servant of the Bois family

Charles, the court wrestler
The Duke Senior
Duke Frederick, the younger Duke
Rosalind/Ganymede, Duke Senior's daughter
Celia/Aliena, the younger Duke's daughter
Monsieur Le Beau, a young courtier
Touchstone, Duke Senior's jester
Corin, a shepherd
Silvius, a shepherd in love with Phebe
Phebe, a disdainful shepherdess
Jacques, the Senior Duke's melancholy follower
Hymen, the God of Marriage

There were once three brothers—Oliver, Orlando and Jacques, the sons of the late Sir Rowland de Bois. Oliver, the eldest had inherited almost all his father's property. While it was not clear what the second son had inherited, the young Orlando received only a small sum of a thousand crowns.

Oliver, the eldest, was prejudiced against the handsome Orlando. He neglected his education and treated him shabbily. On the other hand, he sent his middle brother, Jacques, to school. Orlando had reached the end of his tether and was ready to mutiny against the unfairness of his brother, a fact that he mentioned to his father's loyal old servant, Adam.

When Oliver approached Orlando, the latter expressed his resentment against the way his elder brother was treating him. He raised a hand against him and demanded that Oliver give him what their father had bequeathed to him.

'You shall hear me. My father charged you in his will to give me good education: you have trained me like a peasant, obscuring and hiding from me all gentleman-like qualities.'

Since Orlando was the stronger of the two, Oliver agreed to give him his portion, and told him to leave, along with Adam whom he referred to as 'old dog'.

After they left, Oliver met Charles, the court wrestler, and asked him for news from the court. Charles informed him that the old Duke had been banished to the forest of Arden by the younger Duke, Frederick. Some of the old Duke's loyal noblemen had also left with him, and their lands had been usurped by Frederick.

'There's no news at the court, sir, but the old news: that is, the old duke is banished by his younger brother the new duke.'

Oliver was keen to know if Rosalind, the old Duke's daughter, had also left with her father. Charles replied that Rosalind had remained at court because Duke Frederick loved her like his own daughter. Besides, Frederick's daughter, Celia, and Rosalind had grown up together and could not stay without each other.

Charles had also heard that, in a wrestling bout to be held the next day, Orlando was planning to disguise himself and wrestle against him. He had come to ask Oliver to dissuade his brother from doing so, because Charles did not want to hurt the young man.

However, Oliver who was jealous of his younger brother's popularity, persuaded Charles that Orlando was a cunning villain who was plotting against him.

*'I assure thee, and almost with tears I speak it, there is not
one so young and so villainous this day living.'*

He even told Charles that Orlando would not hesitate to
poison him or entrap him in some way. Charles believed
Oliver blindly and assured him that he would repay
Orlando in his own coin.

Rosalind and Celia were sitting on the lawn outside
the Duke's palace. Rosalind was heavy-hearted after
her father's banishment and Celia tried to cheer her up
by promising her that, after her own father's death, she
would compensate Rosalind by restoring everything taken
from her. While they were talking, Monsieur Le Beau, a
young courtier, came in to tell them about the wrestling
match that would show off the prowess of Charles, the
court wrestler. The young ladies decided to witness
the wrestling.

Duke Frederick entered at that moment and asked his
daughter and her cousin to speak to a certain young man
who had challenged the powerful Charles to a wrestling
match. The two ladies tried their best to dissuade the
handsome young man, who happened to be Orlando, from
the challenge, but he refused to listen. Both wished him
well and hoped that he would be able to hold his own.

Much to everyone's astonishment, Orlando defeated
Charles. Duke Frederick was impressed, but the moment
he heard that Orlando was the son of Sir Rowland, he
realized that he was the son of his enemy.

'I would thou hadst been son to some man else:
The world esteem'd thy father honourable,
But I did find him still mine enemy:

Thou shouldst have better pleased me with this deed,
Hadst thou descended from another house.'

Celia and Rosalind congratulated Orlando. Rosalind told him how much her father admired his father. Orlando was smitten by Rosalind even though he did not know who she was. It was only later that Le Beau told him that she was the banished Duke's daughter. He added that Duke Frederick, who loved Rosalind as much as his own daughter, was slowly getting infuriated by people praising her virtues.

Rosalind spoke of her admiration for Orlando to Celia. As they were conversing, an enraged Duke Frederick came there and told Rosalind that he was banishing her for being a traitor. He warned her that if she were found within twenty miles of his court, she would be put to death. When she protested that she was no traitor, he said angrily,

'Thou art thy father's daughter; there's enough.'

Rosalind reminded him that when he had usurped her father's kingdom and banished him, she had still been her father's daughter. When Celia tried to intercede, her father did not listen. Celia insisted that she and Rosalind were inseparable and that she could not live without her.

The Duke remarked that Rosalind was subtle and sweet, and the people loved and pitied her for these qualities. To Celia, he said,

'Thou are a fool; she robs thee of thy name;
And thou wilt show more bright and seem more virtuous
When she is gone.'

However, Celia was unwilling to heed her father's words. Once he had left, she told Rosalind that her father had banished her as well because she could not imagine being parted from her cousin. She asked Rosalind not to lose heart.

> *'Prithee be cheerful: know'st thou not, the duke*
> *Hath banish'd me, his daughter?'*
>
> Rosalind: *'That he hath not.'*
>
> Celia: *'No, hath not? Rosalind lacks then the love*
> *Which teacheth thee that thou and I am one:*
> *Shall we be sunder'd? Shall we part, sweet girl?*
> *No: let my father seek another heir.'*

They decided to steal away to the Forest of Arden. Since it was unsafe for two young gentlewomen to travel on their own, Rosalind decided to disguise herself as a young man, Ganymede, while Celia would dress as a common maid and call herself Aliena. They would ask the fool, Touchstone, to escort them into the forest.

Meanwhile, the senior Duke, Rosalind's father, had become quite accustomed to the hard life in the forest. He preferred it to the painted pomp and vanity of the court and quoted,

> *'Sweet are the uses of adversity,*
> *Which like the toad, ugly and venomous,*
> *Wears yet a precious jewel in his head.'*

He did not want to change anything of his present circumstances, because the woods offered him everything that he needed to lead a good life, though he did lament over the unfairness of hunting the native deer in their very own homes.

Duke Frederick was enraged to find his daughter and his niece missing. When he heard that the two ladies had been complimenting Orlando, he surmised that they had gone away with him. He ordered his men to bring Oliver to him. He would recruit him to find his brother, Orlando, and the two ladies. When Oliver appeared before him, Duke Frederick ordered him to find his brother within a year. If not, his lands and property would be seized from him.

Orlando had reached home after his victory over Charles. As he was about to enter the house, he was stopped by Adam, the old servant, who warned him that his bravery and his strength had proved to be his enemies. His brother, Oliver, jealous of him, had made plans to burn the place where he slept, and him, that very night. Adam requested Orlando to go away. When Orlando replied that he would have to beg or rob to make a living, the generous Adam offered him the five hundred crowns that he had saved up in his service. He also asked him to take him along so that he could serve him.

Rosalind as Ganymede, Celia as Aliena, and Touchstone, the fool, reached the Forest of Arden, exhausted and hungry. They overheard the conversation of two shepherds, Corin and Silvius, the latter confessing his undying love for the shepherdess Phebe. After Silvius wandered off, Touchstone asked Corin if they could find a place to rest. Corin spoke of his churlish master whose modest property was on sale. Having fallen in love with the place, the two ladies decided to buy it.

Orlando and Adam had also made their way to the forest. Adam was bone-tired and famished. He exclaimed that he would die of hunger, but Orlando reassured him, saying they he would bear him off to a sheltered place, and then go and look for food for him. Orlando himself was so hungry that he burst into the spot where the Duke senior and his courtiers were conversing and demanded food from them with his sword drawn.

The Duke, who was doubtful whether it was distress or ill breeding that made Orlando so rude, treated him courteously and invited him to share their meal. By then, Orlando had recovered his composure and apologized for his rudeness. He mentioned that he needed to first feed the old man who had followed him loyally and asked the Duke for permission to bring him there.

After he left, the Duke remarked to his melancholy follower, Jacques, that all men had their troubles. Jacques' reply was poetic.

'All the world's a stage,
And all the men and women merely players:
They have their exits and their entrances;
And one man in his time plays many parts,
His acts being seven ages.'

Orlando returned soon after, leading the exhausted Adam in. The Duke invited them to sup with him. He welcomed Orlando warmly when he heard that he was his dear friend, Sir Rowland's son, and they supped together.

Meanwhile, Orlando, who had fallen in love with Rosalind, wrote verses of love, hanging them on every tree. Rosalind who was disguised as Ganymede, read them and wondered who was singing her praises so lavishly.

Celia, as Aliena, confided in her that it was Orlando who was writing them. Rosalind, as Ganymede, tackled Orlando, who admitted that he was the one writing verses for Rosalind. Ganymede taunted him, remarking that nothing in his appearance or his manner distinguished him as a man in love.

When Orlando insisted that he was very much in love, Ganymede offered him a cure. He told him that he was to woo him, Ganymede, as though he were Rosalind.

'I would cure you, if you would but call me Rosalind
And come every day to my cote and woo me.'

Rosalind had also lost her heart to Orlando. She spoke of her love to Celia. The Senior Duke, who had met her as Ganymede, had asked her about her parentage, and she had mentioned that her parentage was as noble as his own was. Little did he suspect that she was his own daughter.

Meanwhile, the above-mentioned Silvius, the shepherd, was desperately in love with Phebe, a shepherdess who thought she was above him. The more he declared his love for her, the more disdainful she was towards him. Ganymede heard their conversation and scolded Phebe for being so rude and thoughtless. He told her that she should accept Silvius's suit because she was too plain to get any other offers.

Despite being criticized, Phebe was captivated by Ganymede's magnetic personality. She called him a peevish boy and yet, a pretty youth. She decided to write him a stern letter chiding him for being so impertinent.

By now, Orlando had arrived at their house, an hour late, and Ganymede scolded him pretending to be his

Rosalind. Orlando apologized and spoke of his love, while Ganymede teased him and spurned him. Finally, Ganymede requested Aliena to act as a priest and marry them. When Orlando declared that he would love Rosalind forever and a day, Ganymede replied,

> *'No, no, Orlando; men are April when they woo,*
> *December when they wed:*
> *Maids are May when they are maids, but the sky changes*
> *When they are wives.'*

Orlando then excused himself as he had to meet the Senior Duke for a meal, but he promised to be back soon. After he had left, Celia accused her cousin of having maligned all women, but Rosalind replied that she was a little mad because she was deeply in love and could not bear to be out of Orlando's sight.

At that moment, the poor Silvius arrived with a letter for Ganymede from Phebe. He assumed that it was a letter scolding him, but when he read it aloud, he realized that it was a love letter to himself. Ganymede sent Silvius back to Phebe ordering her to love Silvius instead.

Soon after, a stranger approached them and asked for directions to the cottage where Ganymede and Aliena lived. When he realized that the two people he was seeking were before him, he held out a blood-stained handkerchief to Ganymede from Orlando and described what had befallen the young man. Orlando was passing through the forest, when he came across a wretched man with overgrown hair, asleep under an oak tree. A green and gold snake had wound itself around his neck, and would have entered the man's mouth, if Orlando had not disturbed it.

Immediately, the snake crawled towards a bush, where a hungry lioness crouched, waiting for the man to wake up so that she could pounce on him. By then, Orlando had recognized the man as his elder brother Oliver, a brother whom he considered the most inhumane man alive. He had a mind to leave him to his fate, but being a kind and good man, he fought the lioness and overcame her. His brother heard the commotion and awoke.

Rosalind was more concerned about the blood-stained handkerchief. The man continued with his account. He confessed that he was Oliver, the evil brother who had tried to kill Orlando. However, he had now turned over a new leaf. After the brothers had been reconciled, Orlando took him to the Duke Senior who gave him fresh clothes. When they went to Orlando's cave, Oliver saw blood gushing from his brother's arm from where the lioness had gored him. He had been bleeding all the while, and now he fainted, calling out Rosalind's name. When he regained consciousness, he sent Oliver with the handkerchief stained with his blood to the youth he jokingly called Rosalind so that he might relate the story and apologize for being late once again.

When she heard the whole story, Rosalind fainted. When she regained consciousness, she insisted that her swoon was just an act, since she was pretending to be Rosalind. Oliver was not convinced as she looked pale, and he waited for an answer from her to his brother. She said she would devise an answer but that he would have to tell Orlando how well she had pretended to faint.

The strangest thing had happened. Oliver and Aliena had fallen in love at first sight. He wooed her and she agreed to marry him. Orlando, who was astonished, gave them his consent. He declared that they could be married the very next day in the presence of the Duke and his followers.

> *'I love Aliena; say with her that she loves me;*
> *consent with both that we may enjoy each other: it*
> *shall be to your good; for my father's house and all*
> *the revenue that was old Sir Rowland's will I*
> *estate upon you, and here live and die a shepherd.'*

Orlando was happy for his brother, but he was also bitter about seeing happiness through another man's eyes. He confided in Ganymede that his heart would break when he saw how happy his brother was, and how unhappy he himself was.

Ganymede comforted him saying that he had special magical powers, having been in touch with a powerful magician since the age of three. He promised that if Orlando loved Rosalind with all his heart, he, Ganymede, would ensure that, at the very moment when Oliver married Aliena, Orlando would marry Rosalind.

Orlando could not believe his ears. He asked Ganymede if he was serious, and he replied,

> *'Put you in your best array, bid your friends, for if you*
> *will be married tomorrow, you shall, and to Rosalind,*
> *if you will.'*

Meanwhile, Silvius and Phebe reached there. It was a comic scene with Silvius talking of his love for Phebe, Phebe in love with Ganymede and Orlando talking of his love for Rosalind. Finally, Ganymede satisfied them all by promising that they would all get their hearts' desire. He asked them all to meet there the next day.

When the next day dawned, the Duke Senior and a few men reached the spot, along with Orlando, Oliver and Celia. The Duke was curious to see if the boy, Ganymede, could perform the miracles that he had promised. Just then, Ganymede entered, followed by Silvius and Phebe. He turned to the Duke Senior and asked,

'You say, if I bring in your Rosalind.
You will bestow her on Orlando here?'

The Duke conceded that he would even if he had whole kingdoms to give along with her.

Next, Ganymede asked Orlando whether he would accept Rosalind, and he said he would even if he were the king of all kingdoms.

Ganymede continued his questioning asking Phebe if she would marry the faithful Silvius if she found that she could not marry Ganymede for some reason and Phebe agreed. Silvius also replied that he would marry Phebe even if he were to die immediately after.

Having confirmed all these facts, Ganymede remarked,

'I have promised to make all this matter even.'

He and Aliena left, promising to be back soon.

After they left, the Duke Senior remarked that the young lad reminded him of his daughter, Rosalind. Orlando added on to that, saying that when he first met Ganymede, he had thought he was Rosalind's brother.

In the end, Rosalind and Celia returned, dressed as themselves, having bade goodbye to Ganymede and Aliena. They were accompanied by Hymen, the god of marriage, as soft music played. Hymen presented Rosalind to her father, the Duke Senior, saying that he had brought her from heaven so that she might be united with the man she loved.

Rosalind addressed her father first.

'To you I give myself, for I am yours.'

Then, she turned to Orlando with the same words.

'To you I give myself, for I am yours.'

Both were elated, and the Duke welcomed his daughter and his niece with equal pleasure. The confusion being now resolved, Hymen sang a wedlock song to celebrate the union of the young couples present there.

At that moment, the middle son of Sir Rowland, Jacques de Bois, reached there with more good news. The envious Duke Frederick had come to the forest of Arden to capture his banished brother. At the edge of the forest, he came across an old religious man and began a conversation with him, at the end of which, he was quite converted. He was filled with remorse and decided to retire from the world. Before he did that, he restored all the lands that he had usurped from his brother and others.

The Duke welcomed the young man and commended him for having brought wedding presents to both his brothers, Oliver and Orlando. Oliver would get back his lands and Orlando would inherit the Duke Senior's dukedom. This news was happily received by the Duke Senior who proclaimed that he would share his newly acquired wealth with all those who had been part of his life and retinue in the forest.

Thus, the story having ended well, with all the couples having been united, and honours being restored, it was time to celebrate with music and revelry.

Brief Note

As You Like It is one of the popular pastoral comedies of William Shakespeare. It was written in the years between 1598 and 1600 and published in 1623 in the First Folio, which is the collected edition of the Bard's plays. The play was set in France and the Forest of Arden. Rosalind, the heroine, is considered as one of the most inspiring creations of the Bard, with more lines than any of his other female characters. This is surprising because the writing of the play coincided with the end of Queen Elizabeth's reign, an era when England was highly patriarchal. Women's rights were few and far between, and most marriages were arranged. There was no question of women following their own free will and marrying for love, a state which was frowned upon. Thus, there were strictures and rules, both for royalty and for commoners.

Given this context, Shakespeare went against the grain when he wrote this delightful pastoral story where people co-existed with Mother Nature, living serene lives in forests. They met, fell in love and married one another, living thereafter in perfect bliss.

Stranger is the fact that, in those days, women's parts were often played by young boys. Hence, Rosalind, a boy, would have acted as a girl, and later on as Ganymede, a young boy, that is a boy actor impersonating a girl disguised as a boy.

The themes of love at first sight, the variation between court and country life, the theme of gender, injustice and forgiveness are all highlighted in this play which was considered a crowd puller. It was replete with songs and music and the melancholic Jacques has garnered quite a fan following over the centuries with his famous quotes, especially the loved 'All's the World's a Stage' which is considered one of the most famous monologues of all times.

This play has been performed countless times, having been adapted to the radio, theatre and the silver screen as well.

7

TWELFTH NIGHT/WHAT YOU WILL

7.1: *Twelfth Night.*
Artist: Vrindha Nair.

Characters in the Order of their Appearance

Duke Orsino of Illyria
Lady Olivia

**Viola/Cesario, a gentle lady who disguises herself
as a young man
Sebastian, Viola's brother
The Captain
Sir Toby Belch, a gentleman
Sir Andrew Aguecheek, Olivia's inane suitor
Antonio, a ship Captain
Officers of the Duke**

Duke Orsino, who lived in Illyria, was in love with the beautiful Lady Olivia, who did not return his affection. The lovesick Duke ordered his musicians to entertain him.

> *'Give me excess of it, that, surfeiting,*
> *The appetite may sicken, and so die.*
> *If music be the food of love, play on.'*

He even refused to go hunting, a favourite pastime of his, preferring to lie on a bed of flowers and dream of his lady love.

Lady Olivia, who had lost her father a year ago, was again in mourning after the recent death of her beloved brother. She had vowed to veil her face and keep away from the company of men for seven years.

Meanwhile, a ship was wrecked off the coast of Illyria in a violent storm. A young gentle lady named Viola had been rescued. Her brother, Sebastian, had also been on the boat. She asked the Captain of the ship whether Sebastian had survived as well. The Captain assured her that he had seen him clinging on to a broken mast and he hoped that he was safe.

Left alone in a strange place, Viola asked the Captain about the ruler of the land. The Captain regaled her with the saga of Duke Orsino and his one-sided love for Lady Olivia. Viola decided to disguise herself as a young man and enter the service of the Duke till she found another way to sustain herself.

Olivia's uncle, Sir Toby Belch, and his foolish friend, Sir Andrew Aguecheek, were entertaining themselves at Olivia's house with drunken revels and horseplay. Sir Andrew hoped to woo Olivia and Sir Toby encouraged him saying that Olivia would never marry anyone above her status. Thus, there was hope for the foolish gentleman.

Viola was now disguised as a young man, Cesario. She endeared herself to the Duke in just three days. The Duke was confident that Cesario was the right person, handsome and young, to carry his messages of love to Olivia. Viola agreed to do so reluctantly as she had fallen in love with him. She whispered to herself,

'I'll do my best
To woo your lady:

(Aside)

yet, a barful strife!
Whoe'er I woo, myself would be his wife.'

Olivia received the message that a young man was waiting at her gate to meet her. She did not want to see him, but Cesario refused to leave without giving her the message from his master. Olivia finally let him in, and she was impressed with his graceful and handsome looks. She refused to let Cesario finish his master's message and instead asked him about his own parentage, to which he replied,

'*Above my fortunes, yet my state is well:*
I am a gentleman.'

When he left, she sent a ring after him as a token of her interest in him, for she had fallen in love with him.

When Cesario/Viola saw the ring, she realized that, perhaps, Olivia had fallen in love with her outward appearance. How ironic it was that the lady had fallen for another lady, dressed in man's clothing! By now, Viola herself had fallen in love with Duke Orsino. It was too difficult a tangle to be sorted out. She shuddered to think of the complications that lay ahead of her. She said to herself,

'*O time! Thou must untangle this, not I;*
It is too hard a knot for me to untie.'

The next day, Orsino told Cesario that he seemed to be in love. He gave him some advice on love and then told him to go back to Olivia, this time carrying a jewel from him. When Cesario went back to Olivia to talk of the Duke's love again, Olivia confessed that she had fallen in love with the messenger, and not the master. Viola, as Cesario, told her openly that no woman would be mistress of her heart, going on to suggest,

'*I am not what I am.*'

As Cesario was about to leave, Olivia begged him to come back again, claiming,

'*Love sought is good, but given unsought is better.*'

Meanwhile, a captain named Antonio had rescued Sebastian and tended to him till he recovered. Sebastian had no idea that his sister, Viola, had also survived the shipwreck. He assumed that he had no one in the world and had decided to go to Duke Orsino's house to find his fortune. He and Antonio soon reached Illyria, where Antonio generously handed over his purse to Sebastian who wanted to see the sights of the town.

Cesario was once again at Olivia's door. This time, Olivia gave him a locket with her picture in it. Sir Andrew, who fancied himself in love with Olivia, egged on by Sir Tony, challenged the timid Cesario to a duel. As they drew their swords, Antonio turned up and mistook Cesario for Sebastian. He offered to fight the duel in his place, but at that very moment, a few officers burst in and arrested Antonio, who had been in trouble with the Duke some years ago. Antonio knew that he would need some money to clear his name. When he asked Cesario, mistaking him for Sebastian, about the money he had given him earlier, Cesario told him that neither had he received any money from him, nor did he recognize him. Antonio was led away, protesting at Sebastian's ingratitude, leaving Viola with the hope that, maybe, her beloved brother was still alive.

The confusion continued, unabated, as Sebastian found himself at Olivia's house, where Sir Toby, taking him for Cesario, attacked him. Sebastian, who had no idea why he was being attacked, drew his sword, but before they could launch into a duel, Olivia came rushing in to prevent the fight. When she lovingly addressed him as Cesario, Sebastian wondered if he were dreaming and exclaimed,

'If it be thus to dream, still let me sleep.'

He wished he could discuss it with Antonio who seemed to have disappeared. Olivia had even brought along a priest so that they could get married, because she did not want Cesario to change his mind. A bewildered Sebastian happily agreed, and the priest conducted their wedding.

Orsino, who had got tired of waiting for Olivia to respond to his overtures, decided to go to her house, accompanied by his faithful Cesario. The officers who had arrested Antonio came looking for Orsino, and again, Antonio accused Cesario, whom he called Sebastian, of betraying him by not recognizing him or returning his purse to him, the purse he had handed over to him just that morning.

> *'A witchcraft drew me hither:*
> *That most ingrateful boy there by your side,*
> *From the rude sea's enraged and foamy mouth*
> *Did I redeem; a wreck past hope he was.'*

The Duke stepped in. He asked Antonio when he and Sebastian had come to Illyria. When Antonio replied that they had got there that morning, Orsino explained that it was impossible since Cesario had been serving him for the past three months.

At that moment, Olivia came into the room. Upon seeing Cesario, she referred to him as 'husband'. She upbraided him for deserting her, after having married her a few hours earlier. Both Orsino and Cesario were flabbergasted as Olivia summoned the priest who had performed the ceremony as a witness.

Viola/Cesario protested that she loved only her master, which shocked Olivia, who felt betrayed by the man she thought she had married. An affronted Orsino peremptorily warned Olivia and Cesario never to come before him ever again.

To add to the mayhem, Sir Andrew hobbled in, asking for a doctor as he and Sir Toby had been injured in a fight with Cesario, which was again denied by him.

At that moment, Sebastian appeared. As everyone gaped at him, he greeted Antonio happily. Only then did they understand that Viola and Sebastian were identical twins and had both survived the shipwreck. Orsino voiced his thoughts.

'One face, one voice, one habit, and two persons,
A natural perspective, that is and is not!'

The twins' happiness at having found each other again knew no bounds.

When Orsino realized that Olivia was married to Sebastian, it took him no time to rally around. He realized that his faithful Cesario was, in reality, a woman named Viola. He asked her if she had meant all her proclamations of love towards him. He added that he wanted to see her in her own clothes, which she had left in safety with the sea captain who had rescued her. It took him no time to transfer his affection to Viola, especially after he saw her in woman's clothing.

Orsino also declared that a double wedding would soon be held in Illyria, celebrating his love for Viola, and that of the Lady Olivia and Sebastian, thus ending all the confusion that had surrounded them all these days.

7.2: *Twelfth Night.*
Artist: Leah Teresa Chakola.

Brief Note

Twelfth Night was written between 1600 and 1602 and printed in the First Folio of 1623. A comedy in five acts, *Twelfth Night* had all the elements of a good entertainer.

Twelfth Night referred to the 6th of January, the twelfth night after Christmas, a Christian holiday which was, therefore, an occasion for feasting and revelry. This play was written by Shakespeare to be staged twelve days after Christmas before Queen Elizabeth I. A romantic comedy, the play's themes included love, both romantic and unrequited, sorrow, deception and disguise, cross dressing, the folly of ambition and class hierarchy. There was a marked difference between appearance and reality.

This is considered one of the Bard's most modern plays. Many later writers were influenced by lines from the play. Arthur Conan Doyle made Sherlock Holmes quote twice from *Twelfth Night*, which made certain readers believe that Holmes' birthday fell on the 6th of January. The Queen of Mystery, Agatha Christie, derived the title of one of her popular novels, *Sad Cypress* from the song in Act II, Scene IV of *Twelfth Night*.

8

KING LEAR

8.1: *King Lear.*
Artist: S.K. Riyazul Rahaman.

Characters in the Order of their Appearance

King Lear
Goneril, Lear's eldest daughter
Regan, Lear's middle daughter
Cordelia, Lear's youngest daughter

The Duke of Cornwall, Regan's husband
The Duke of Albany, Goneril's husband
The Earl of Kent/Caius
The King of Burgundy
The King of France, Cordelia's husband
The Earl of Gloucester
Edmund, Gloucester's elder son
Edgar/Poor Tom, Gloucester's younger son
Oswald, Goneril's manservant
Fool, faithful jester to Lear
Knight
Gloucester's Tenant

King Lear was growing old. He desired to divide his kingdom among his three daughters, Goneril, Regan and Cordelia. He also wanted to spend his last days with his children and absolve himself of the responsibilities of kingship. As his three daughters stood before him, he asked them to prove how much each loved him, for he would divide his kingdom based on who loved him most.

Goneril and Regan were wonderful flatterers and they let their tongues run away with descriptions of their love. The king was ecstatic, and he gave them both one third of his kingdom. He waited for his favourite daughter, Cordelia, to express her love.

Cordelia was made of different stuff. Though she loved her father dearly, she would not flatter him like her sisters did. Her reply to him was simple.

'I love your majesty
According to my bond; no more no less.'

She continued,

> *'Good my lord,*
> *You have begot me, bred me, loved me: I*
> *Return those duties back as are right fit,*
> *Obey you, love you, and most honour you.'*

King Lear asked her to elaborate on her answer if she wanted to improve her fortunes. Cordelia remained unmoved. She said that she loved him as a daughter for having fathered her and brought her up. However, she refused to say that all her love was for him, as her sisters had proclaimed, for that meant that they had no love left over for their husbands. The man who married her would have half her heart.

King Lear was enraged to hear this. He exclaimed,

> *'So young, and so untender?'*

He disowned Cordelia for having spoken thus and banished her from the kingdom. He divided the third part of his kingdom between his elder daughters and their husbands, the dukes of Cornwall and Albany.

The wise Earl of Kent, who considered the king his patron, warned him that it was unwise to be taken in by flattery. He added that the king's youngest daughter, Cordelia, loved him dearly. Kent was not afraid of speaking his mind.

> *'What wilt thou do, old man?*
> *Think'st thou that duty shall have dread to speak,*
> *When power to flattery bows?'*

However, old Lear refused to see reason and finally, he got so enraged that he banished Kent as well.

The Kings of France and Burgundy were both rivals for Cordelia's hand. When Burgundy heard that Lear had disowned Cordelia and left her without a fortune, he backed away from his proposal. The King of France, however, stood staunch and said that Cordelia was herself a dowry and accepted her as the queen of his heart. King Lear refused to even give her his blessing as she prepared to leave with her suitor. He said in disdain,

'Thou hast her, France: let her be thine, for we
Have no such daughter, nor shall ever see
That face of hers again.'

Left alone with her sisters, the tender-hearted Cordelia pleaded with them to treat their father well, and they spurned her advice in disdain, telling her to take care of her own situation. After she left, the two sisters conferred between themselves, speaking of their father's erratic behaviour.

''Tis the infirmity of his age: yet he hath ever
but slenderly known himself.'

They were aware that they would have to endure further unpredictable decisions made by him in his old age and that they would have to curb his authority. Obviously, they were not in the least impressed with his great generosity towards them.

Elsewhere in the kingdom as well, intrigue reigned supreme.

The Earl of Gloucester, one of Lear's subjects, had two sons, Edmund and Edgar. Edmund was jealous of Edgar, the Earl's legitimate son, and wanted to get rid of him so that he could usurp his father's title and power. Gloucester was caught unawares by a fake letter written by Edgar, in which he spoke about wanting to destroy him and take his power. Edmund had forged this letter to influence his father against his younger son.

He pretended to hide it from his father, saying,

'I beseech you, sir, pardon me: it is a letter
from my brother, that I have not all o'er-read;
and for so much as I have perused, I find it not
fit for your o'er-looking.'

In turn, he told Edgar that their father was angry with him because someone had filled his ears against him. Thus, he played one against the other. A heartbroken Gloucester, who loved Edgar dearly, banished him from his sight.

Meanwhile, Lear lived with Goneril, his eldest daughter, for a month. She was unhappy about the hundred riotous knights he had with him. Besides, she could not stand being ruled over by him anymore, especially since he had given away his authority. She said in contempt,

'Idle old man,
That still would manage those authorities
That he hath given away.'

She ordered her servants to neglect her father's needs and be rude to him. If he lost his temper, she would send him to her sister, Regan, before the month ended.

The loyal Earl of Kent, who had earlier been banished by Lear, disguised himself as a commoner called Caius, so that he could still serve the old king. When Goneril's man, Oswald, behaved rudely to Lear, Kent stepped in to trip him up. He thus gained Lear's confidence and offered him his services. At that moment, an infuriated Goneril came in and told Lear that his knights and servants were so disorderly that she planned to send half of them away. Lear was aghast and rued the day that he had handed over his land and power to her. Albany, Goneril's husband, tried to curb her, but she refused to listen. Lear was helpless, and he cried out,

'How sharper than a serpent's tooth it is
To have a thankless child.'

He cursed Goneril, proclaiming that he still had a kind daughter who would take him in and help him to regain his lost power. In a rage, he left Goneril's court for good, looking forward to being with his second daughter.

Meanwhile, Goneril wrote a letter to her sister, warning her of their father's arrival, knowing fully well that Regan would also not allow him to keep a hundred knights at her home.

Whenever Lear lost his temper and acted imperiously, it was his faithful fool who kept his spirits high and added sly asides on how foolish the old man had been to give away his kingdom and his power to his two daughters. Lear, whose mind was failing him, knew that the fool was right. He exclaimed,

'O, let me not be mad, not mad, sweet heaven
Keep me in temper: I would not be mad!'

Meanwhile, Edmund was still acting deceitful, playing off his guileless brother, Edgar, against his father, Gloucester. Having told Edgar that his father was angry and planning to act against him, he advised him to flee and keep himself hidden. Once Edgar had left, Edmund wounded himself with his sword, cutting his arm.

'Some blood drawn on me would beget opinion.'

He pretended that Edgar had inflicted it on him because he, Edmund, had refused to help him to murder their father. Gloucester was gullible enough to believe his false son and decided to hunt Edgar down and punish him severely.

The Earl of Kent, in disguise as Caius, landed up at Gloucester's castle and quarrelled with Oswald, Goneril's servant, who had accompanied his mistress there. For that, he was punished and tied down in the stocks (a wooden device that shackled a person's ankles so that he could not move).

As he dozed, Edgar came in, on the run from those who hunted him. He covered his face with dirt and ripped his fine clothes. He would pretend to be 'poor Tom', a beggar who had escaped from an asylum, for his own safety.

Lear too had made his way to Gloucester's castle where he was shocked to find his servant, Caius, Kent in disguise, in the stocks. He could not believe that this was the doing of his daughter, Regan, and her husband, who had received a letter from Goneril, warning them about Lear's unreasonable behaviour. He demanded to meet them both.

'The king would speak with Cornwall; the dear father
Would with his daughter speak, commands her service.'

When Lear came face to face with Regan and Cornwall, he complained bitterly against his oldest daughter and her treatment of him. However, he was shattered when Goneril also arrived and both his daughters allied themselves against him, calling him old and weak. They brought down his number of men to fifty, then twenty-five and at the end, left him with no servants at all.

Lear was in a flaming rage and he cursed his daughters, swearing that he would have revenge on them.

> *'You heavens, give me that patience, patience I need!*
> *You see me here, you gods, a poor old man,*
> *As full of grief as age; wretched in both!*
> *If it be you that stir these daughters' hearts*
> *Against their father, fool me not so much*
> *To bear it tamely; touch me with noble anger,*
> *And let not women's weapons, water-drops,*
> *Stain my man's cheeks!'*

Thus saying, he strode outside where a dreadful storm was brewing. His daughters did not try to stop him and closed the door against him.

Kent who had now been freed, went after the king, but came across a knight of his instead. He told him to go to Dover where he would find support for Lear. He handed over a ring to be given to Cordelia, who would recognize who had sent the knight. The two of them then went in opposite directions, trying to find the king.

Lear and his fool wandered along the heath, buffeted by the storm. The old man raved against the elements, following it up with curses against his ungrateful daughters. It was there that Kent found them and pleaded with them to get out of the storm. Lear continued to rail against the storm, but finally ended his words on a poignant note.

> *'I am a man*
> *More sinn'd against than sinning.'*

Kent led them to a hovel where they could take shelter against the storm. Lear refused to go in, still heartbroken. He cried,

> *'In such a night*
> *To shut me out! Pour on; I will endure.*
> *O Regan, Goneril!*
> *Your kind old father, whose frank heart gave all.'*

He sent Kent and the fool into the hovel and prepared to pray. The fool went in and came charging out, crying that there was a spirit within. The spirit was none other

8.2: *King Lear.*
Artist: Aditya Sujith.

than Edgar, disguised as poor Tom, who pretended to be mad. Lear conversed with him, tearing his own clothes in sympathy. At that moment, Gloucester came in with a flaming torch, looking for the old king.

The Duke of Gloucester, who was good at heart, did not approve of turning the old king out, but he was cut short by Regan and Cornwall. He informed his son, Edmund, of a secret letter about an invading French army that had come to the aid of King Lear. He asked his son to distract the duke of Cornwall so that he himself could steal away and seek out the helpless old king. The treacherous Edmund immediately betrayed his father to Cornwall in order to inherit his wealth and his power.

Gloucester took the deranged king, the fool, Kent and Edgar both in disguise, to a safe chamber away from the storm. He left them there, only to return post haste, to warn them about a plot of death against Lear. He told them to transport Lear to Dover where he would be protected by friends. Edgar mused over how little he had suffered when compared to the king's greater ordeals.

'When we our betters see bearing our woes,
We scarcely think our miseries our foes.'

Even as Lear was taken to safety, Gloucester was taken captive and questioned by Cornwall and the wicked daughters of Lear. When he spoke up for Lear, his eyes were put out, and he was thrown out of his own castle, defenceless and blind.

The blind Gloucester's heart bled when he realized that his elder son, Edmund, had betrayed him. His old tenant found him wandering about on the heath. He

8.3: *King Lear.*
Artist: Binitta Biffin.

walked along with him and they came across Edgar who was heartbroken to see the plight of his poor father. Gloucester asked Edgar, who was still disguised as poor Tom, to lead him to Dover. Edgar was still overcome. He said to himself,

'The worst is not
So long as we can say, "This is the worst."'

Gloucester missed his son, Edgar, whom he had wronged, and he found himself thinking of him when he heard poor Tom speak. He said philosophically,

'As flies to wanton boys, are we to the gods
They kill us for their sport.'

He requested Edgar to lead him to the edge of the high cliffs of Dover, from where he would not need anyone to lead him further. Edgar took Gloucester there, pretending that they had reached the high cliffs. Gloucester believed him. He prayed to the gods and jumped, but he did not fall far. Edgar assured him that since he had survived his fall, the very gods wanted him to live.

Goneril's husband, the Duke of Albany, had seen through her treatment of her father and was disgusted with her actions. He condemned her and called her a monster. Just then, a messenger came in and informed them that the Duke of Cornwall, Regan's husband, had died of a sword wound inflicted by a loyal servant of Gloucester's.

Meanwhile, several other events were taking place. Albany, a true gentleman, was shocked at how Edmund had betrayed his own father. He vowed to take revenge on him.

Kent, who was at the French camp at Dover, heard that Cordelia had received his letters regarding her father's plight and had wept over them, according to the gentleman who had carried them to her.

'Faith, once or twice she heaved the name of "father"
Pantingly forth, as if it press'd her heart:
Cried" 'Sisters! sisters! Shame of ladies! sisters!
Kent! father! sisters! What, i' the storm? i' the night?
Let pity not be believed!"'

Lear, who was wavering between sanity and lunacy, was now in Dover, but refused to meet his youngest daughter, ashamed of the way he had disinherited her and given her share of property away to her sisters.

The King of France had gone back to his country on some urgent business. Hence, Cordelia, as the Queen, was in charge of the French army. She sent a hundred soldiers to search for her poor insane father who sang as he wandered about, having adorned himself with flowers. She received the news that the British armies were marching against them and her army prepared itself to fight them.

At that moment, Lear wandered by, adorned with wildflowers, spouting nonsense. Though blind, Gloucester recognized his voice. As they conversed, Cordelia's soldiers came in, looking for the old king. Before they could catch him to lead him safely to Cordelia, he ran away in a frenzy.

Ironically, Goneril and Regan had both set their eyes on marrying Edmund, the future earl of Gloucester. They had sent him letters conveying their intentions. Now, when Oswald, Goneril's man servant, saw Gloucester, he proclaimed him a traitor and set out to kill him. Edgar retaliated and wounded him. Before he died, Oswald requested him to hand over the letter he was carrying to Edmund, the future earl of Gloucester. Edgar opened the letter which revealed Goneril's plot to remove her husband and marry Edmund. Gloucester was downcast. He wished he were insane so that he could be distracted from his grievous sorrows.

Back in the French camp, Lear had been given new garments and been tended to by Cordelia's doctor. After a sound sleep, he awoke, confused about where he was.

As he tried to kneel before Cordelia, she stopped him, asking for his blessing instead. Lear exclaimed that he was not in his senses.

'Pray, do not mock me:
I am a very foolish fond old man.'

Cordelia treated him with gentleness, her tender heart breaking at his piteous condition. When he recognized his youngest daughter, he was filled with remorse, as he said to her,

'I know you do not love me; for your sisters
Have, as I do remember, done me wrong:
You have some cause, they have not.'

Cordelia assured him that she had no cause to hate him because she had forgiven him for her banishment.

After Cornwall's death, his army was led by Edmund. Goneril's husband, Albany, had decided to fight against the French army even though his sympathies lay with Lear. As he was musing thus, a disguised Edgar came to him and handed over the fateful letter of betrayal written by Goneril to Edmund.

The battle was soon over, and Lear and Cordelia were taken prisoner. Edmund sent them away with a captain, with orders to deal with them. Regan and Goneril bickered over who would marry Edmund, when suddenly Regan was taken ill.

Albany challenged Edmund to a duel calling him a traitor. If anyone had proof that Edmund was a traitor, he would need to appear before them before the trumpet sounded thrice. Edgar appeared and gave his reasons for calling Edmund a traitor. The two fought and finally

Edmund fell, wounded. Goneril tried to plead for him but Albany produced her letter, accusing her of a conspiracy against him, causing her to rush away.

It was time for Edgar to reveal his identity. He spoke of how he had disguised himself as a madman and led his father to safety. Unfortunately, when he did reveal himself to his father, the older gentleman was so overcome with both joy and grief that his weak heart gave way, and he died. Edmund repented, accepting that he had been treacherous.

> *'Thou hast spoken right; 'tis true;*
> *The wheel is come full circle: I am here.'*

Edgar also mentioned how loyal Kent had been to the old king even though he had been wronged by him.

At that very moment came the disturbing news that Goneril had poisoned her sister, Regan, and ended her own life as well. A repentant Edmund remembered that he had ordered Cordelia's life be ended in the prison. He hurriedly sent his messenger to prevent the heinous act.

Sadly, the damage had already been done, as Lear came in, bearing Cordelia's body. He was overwrought as he tried to check whether there was life in her body.

> *'Howl, howl, howl, howl! O, you are men of stones:*
> *Had I your tongues and eyes, I'd use them so*
> *That heaven's vault should crack. She's gone for ever!*
> *I know when one is dead, and when one lives;*
> *She's dead as earth.'*

Kent came before him, and revealed himself as Caius, his man servant. Lear welcomed him back, but his mind was wandering. Meanwhile, news came in of Edmund's death as well. Lear continued to hover over Cordelia, hoping against hope that she would breathe again, and then, heartbroken, he breathed his last as well.

Albany invited Kent and Edgar to rule with him. Kent did not accept because he felt that he was close to death, but Edgar agreed. Before they all left in a pall of gloom, Albany summed it up by saying poignantly,

'The oldest hath borne most: we that are young
Shall never see so much, nor live so long.'

Thus, ended the poignant saga of King Lear and his three daughters.

Brief Note

William Shakespeare's plays can be divided clearly into comedies, tragedies and histories. *King Lear*, written between 1605 and 1606, is one of his saddest tragedies, divided into five acts. The play revolves around the relationship between an aging father and his daughters, and touches upon the themes of old age, changing family relationships, justice and loyalty and madness and deep sorrow. Ingratitude of children for their parent is a spur that drives the play on. Nature also plays a significant role in this play.

Shakespeare created two distinct types of fools or clowns in his plays. One type depicted natural fools, but many of his fools were placed in the play to narrate universal truths, masked in a tone of folly. They often reflected the customs and the culture of the Elizabethan age through their satiric asides.

Here, Lear's fool was loyal to him, and yet, he never missed an opportunity to remind the old man of how he had allowed his older daughters to hoodwink him.

One of the most famous quotes in *Twelfth Night* is by Feste, who is employed as a fool, but is neither foolish, nor gullible. 'Better a witty fool than a foolish wit.'

King Lear had its fans and its detractors. George Bernard Shaw, himself a notable playwright, had this to say about the Bard and his creation: 'No man will ever write a better tragedy than *Lear*.'

9

MACBETH

9.1: *Macbeth.*
Artist: Vrindha Nair.

Characters in the Order of their Appearance

The Three Witches
Macbeth, an ambitious warrior and lord of Scotland
Duncan, King of Scotland

Banquo, a Scottish nobleman
Lady Macbeth, Macbeth's conniving wife
The Two Chamberlains
Macduff, the Thane of Fife
Malcolm, Duncan's elder son and heir
Donalbain, Duncan's younger son
The Two Murderers
Fleance, Banquo's son

A fierce storm raged over the Scottish moor, as three eerie figures met and danced amidst the thunder and the lightning. They were three witches, haggard and fearsome, who were preparing for their first encounter with Macbeth, a fierce and brave warrior in Scotland, who had won many battles.

'Fair is foul, and foul is fair:
Hover through the fog and filthy air.'

With a shrill screech, they disappeared into the darkness.

Meanwhile, at Forres, Duncan, the Scottish king, had received news of Macbeth, his valiant cousin's victories, over two armies that had threatened Scotland, one against a Scotsman and the other against the army of Norway. The thane of Cawdor, one of the Scottish lords, had been proved a traitor.

Duncan immediately ordered the thane to be put to death and Macbeth to be given the title of Cawdor.

As Macbeth and Banquo, the victors of the recent battle, were making their way to the court, they were suddenly startled by the appearance of the three witches. They looked like women, but they had beards.

The witches hailed Macbeth. Each of them spoke in turn, promising him great honours in the near future.

The first witch whispered, *'All hail, Macbeth! Hail to thee, thane of Glamis.'*

The second witch followed suit, saying, *'All hail, Macbeth! Hail to thee, thane of Cawdor.'*

The third witch had the most startling prophecy. *'All hail, Macbeth! Thou shall be king hereafter.'*

Macbeth was astounded and he wanted to know more.

Banquo was also keen to hear about his future. In turn he asked the three witches,

'If you can look into the seeds of time and say which grain will grow and which will not, speak then unto me.'

The witches prophesied that Banquo would never be king, but that his sons would be future kings of Scotland. They then disappeared into thin air, leaving the two men in utter disbelief.

Immediately after, two men entered and pronounced Macbeth the thane of Cawdor. Since he was the thane of Glamis, two of the prophecies had come already come true. Banquo warned him not to believe too much in the instruments of darkness which could reveal half-truths that could betray them later.

However, the seed had already been planted in Macbeth's mind.

King Duncan received Macbeth and Banquo happily. He thanked them profusely for the heroic way they had fought to uphold the throne. He added that he was going to name his elder son, Malcolm, as the heir to the throne and hoped that all his subjects would be loyal to him. This came as a shock to Macbeth who now realized that Malcolm would be an obstacle in his path towards the throne. He would have to create his own destiny.

'Stars, hide your fires;
Let not light see my black and deep desires:
The eye wink at the hand; yet let that be,
Which the eye fears, when it is done, to see.'

Duncan was so elated that he wanted to honour Macbeth by spending time with him and his wife at his castle in Inverness. Macbeth hurried home to prepare for the arrival of the king, his mind all in turmoil.

Lady Macbeth had just finished reading a letter from her husband in which he spoke of the three prophecies. She was sure of Macbeth's ambition, but she feared that he was not cruel enough to seize the opportunity that was coming their way. She said to herself,

'...yet do I fear thy nature; it is too full o' the milk of
human kindness.'

She had already made up her mind to murder Duncan under their roof. When Macbeth arrived, she greeted him happily. She advised him to welcome Duncan into their home with his eye, his hand and his tongue.

'Look like the innocent flower, but be the serpent under 't.'

Thus, she cleverly began to manipulate her husband's mind towards the murder of his king.

Early next morning, Duncan arrived at Macbeth's castle. As he admired its pleasant environment, Lady Macbeth came out to lead him in with false words of welcome. When Duncan thanked her for her hospitality, she replied that she and her husband owed all that they had to their king.

The evening feast was in full swing when Macbeth took a moment to think about what he was about to do. He felt guilty about plotting to murder Duncan because Macbeth was the king's relative, his subject, and finally, the host who ought to have saved him from murder. Macbeth had almost convinced himself that he would not perform the heinous deed when his wife came looking for him.

The moment Macbeth revealed his doubts, Lady Macbeth accused him of cowardice. She said that this was the perfect opportunity and that they needed to be bold.

'We fail!
But screw your courage to the sticking-place,
And we'll not fail.'

Her nimble brain had already formulated the perfect plan in which they would get the king's chamberlains drunk with wine and smear them with the king's blood so that suspicion would fall on them. Her strong resolve convinced Macbeth to go ahead with their plan.

That night, after Duncan retired to bed, Banquo and Macbeth had a conversation about the three witches. When Macbeth was left alone, he suddenly saw the vision of a dagger floating before him. He could hardly believe his eyes, for the next moment, he imagined drops of blood on the dagger. As he struggled to bring his mind under control, a bell rang signifying that it was time to commit the crime. He stealthily made his way to Duncan's bedchamber.

A little while later, Lady Macbeth came out, waiting for her husband to commit the crime. A noise from within startled her, but soon Macbeth came out, telling her,

'I have done the deed.'

He was shaken because he heard the two chamberlains outside the king's door awaken and pray before they went back to their drunken slumber. In his haste, he had brought with him their two daggers with which he had murdered Duncan. He could not face going back to smear their faces with Duncan's blood. He cried wildly,

'Methought I heard a voice cry, "Sleep no more. Macbeth doth murder sleep."'

He had suddenly realized the immensity of the crime he had committed. Lady Macbeth, who was made of sterner stuff, took the bloodied daggers from him mockingly and went to place them near the sleeping men. There was a knock at the door and the couple rushed into their bedroom to change into their nightgowns, even as Lady Macbeth assured her husband,

'A little water clears us of this deed.'

Early next morning, another knock on the door announced the arrival of Macduff, the Thane of Fife, who had come to rouse the king. The knock woke Macbeth up, and he led Macduff to Duncan's chamber.

In no time, Macduff came running out, crying, *'O horror, horror, horror!'* He had found the king murdered. Lady Macbeth also appeared, pretending to be horrified that such a terrible deed had been done under her roof. The suspicion was put on the chamberlains, but Macbeth killed them in a seeming fit of rage, an act that roused Macduff's suspicions.

In the ensuing chaos, Duncan's sons, Malcolm and Donalbain who had also spent the night there, spoke in whispers, suspecting that they were not safe anymore. Malcolm decided to flee to England while Donalbain would make his way to Ireland. Unfortunately, in the minds of a few, this shifted the suspicion of Duncan's murder on to them.

Meanwhile, Macbeth, who was the next of kin in the absence of the princes, was chosen to be crowned in Duncan's place. By now, Macduff was openly sceptical of Macbeth's innocence in the murder. Instead of attending the coronation, he made his way back to his castle at Fife.

Banquo was still at Macbeth's castle, musing over how the prophecies of the witches had come true for Macbeth. He hoped that he too would benefit by having his sons succeed to the throne after Macbeth. Macbeth was now king, and he and the queen invited Banquo to stay for supper. Banquo told them that he would go for a ride and get back in time for supper.

However, Macbeth had other plans for Banquo, for he now feared him. He arranged for two murderers to accost both Banquo and his son, Fleance, and kill them both. Now that he was king, he did not want Banquo's sons to rule after him, especially since the witches had promised Macbeth a *'fruitless crown'* and *'a barren sceptre'*, which meant that he would have no children.

However, both Macbeth and his wife found no content or peace after having committed the terrible murder. Instead, they found themselves moving apart, especially since Macbeth described his mind as *'full of scorpions'*. He did not tell his wife about his plot to murder Banquo and his son.

That night, as Banquo and Fleance returned to Macbeth's castle, the murderers set upon them. Banquo was killed, but he entreated his son to flee and take revenge on his father's murderers. Macbeth's stroke of luck seemed to have ended with Fleance's escape.

As the guests sat at the supper table laden with a feast, sipping wine, one of the murderers informed the king that, while Banquo had been killed, his son had escaped. Macbeth was horrified and exclaimed,

> *'There the grown serpent lies; the worm that's fled*
> *Hath nature that in time will venom breed.'*

He realized that the young boy could come back and avenge his father's death in the future.

Returning to his guests, he was about to sit down when he caught sight of Banquo's ghost sitting at the table. This horrified him and he spoke wildly to the ghost, who was invisible to the others. Lady Macbeth tried to cover up his strange behaviour. The ghost disappeared, but reappeared when Macbeth spoke Banquo's name. Again, Macbeth started, and spoke to the apparition.

> *'Avaunt! and quit my sight! let the earth hide thee!*
> *Thy bones are marrowless, thy blood is cold;*
> *Thou hast no speculation in those eyes*
> *Which thou dost glare with!'*

Worried that her husband would blurt out all his guilty secrets, Lady Macbeth instantly sent her guests away. Macbeth continued to rave on. He planned to meet the witches again to know more about the future. He was now so steeped in blood that it was impossible to retrace his steps.

Macbeth tried to put the blame of Banquo's death on his son, Fleance. This only served to turn public opinion against Macbeth, who had earlier cast suspicion on Duncan's sons after they fled, following their father's murder. Macduff, who had refused all Macbeth's invitations to the court, was now in England to ask for aid from King Edward to overthrow the tyrant.

Macbeth was desperate to go back to the fearsome witches. He found them on the lonely heath, dancing around the cauldron into which they were throwing in the eye of a newt, the toe of a frog, the wool of a bat and the tongue of a dog, apart from other loathsome ingredients. As they danced, they sang,

'Double, double toil and trouble,
Fire burn, and cauldron bubble.'

Macbeth demanded that they reveal more of his future. The witches cackled and threw more ingredients in the cauldron.

Suddenly, there arose an apparition of the disembodied head of a warrior which warned Macbeth to beware of Macduff's revenge. As Macbeth stared on, the next apparition appeared, revealing a blood-stained baby who prophesied that no man *'born of woman'* could kill Macbeth, which relieved him immensely.

9.2: *Macbeth.*
Artist: Manasa Kalyan.

The last apparition was that of a child wearing a crown. He proclaimed that Macbeth would never be vanquished in battle until Birnam wood moved towards his castle at Dunsinane, something which was physically impossible.

Macbeth had one last query of the witches. He asked them if Banquo's progeny would reign in Scotland after him. The answer was instantaneous. Out of the cauldron appeared a host of future child-kings wearing golden crowns, with Banquo at their head, pointing towards them. The eighth boy-king held up a mirror in which nestled the reflections of many more succeeding kings.

Macbeth was so frustrated at the vision that he cursed the witches, who promptly disappeared. His anger was so potent that when he received the message that Macduff had fled to England, he killed Macduff's wife and young ones. When Macduff heard of this horrific act, he was determined to turn his grief into anger and take revenge on Macbeth.

Lady Macbeth, who had seemed so strong in the beginning, had now begun to sleepwalk, because her mind could not endure the crimes that she and her husband had committed. During her sleepwalking session she referred to the murder of Duncan, exclaiming,

'Yet who would have thought the old man to have so much of blood in him.'

Obviously, the deaths of Lady Macduff and her children, and Banquo, had also affected her mind. She rubbed her hands together frequently, as if she were trying to wash the spots of blood off them, muttering in frustration,

'Here's the smell of the blood still: all the perfumes of Arabia will not sweeten this little hand. Oh, oh, oh!'

Revolts had broken out across Scotland against Macbeth's tyranny. Mortified and angry, he had fortified his castle, but powerful forces were at work against him. The English army led by Malcolm met the Scottish army at Birnam wood, the place mentioned earlier by the witches. Malcolm ordered every soldier to cut a branch and hold it before him while marching to Macbeth's castle, so that their numbers would remain hidden. It was almost as though the prophecy of the witches was coming true, with Birnam Wood appearing to move towards Dunsinane.

Macbeth, meanwhile, had heard reports of ten thousand English soldiers coming to the attack and he was determined to fight them all, bolstered by the false prophecies of the witches. Suddenly, there came a cry from within the castle. Lady Macbeth had passed away. A shocked Macbeth spoke about how time moved on relentlessly towards death. He lamented,

> *'Life's but a walking shadow, a poor player*
> *That struts and frets his hour upon the stage*
> *And then is heard no more: it is a tale*
> *Told by an idiot, full of sound and fury,*
> *Signifying nothing.'*

The next shock was delivered by a messenger who could hardly believe his eyes. He had seen Birnam Wood moving towards Dunsinane, a statement that overwhelmed Macbeth, reminding him of the prophecy. He was now tired of living, but declared that he would go down, fighting.

The battle started and finally, Macduff and Macbeth came, face to face. Macbeth did not want to fight Macduff since he already had the blood of his family on his hands. He warned him that no man born of a woman could kill him.

> *'I bear a charmed life, which must not yield,*
> *To one of woman born.'*

Macduff dashed his hopes by declaring that he was not born of a woman but had been ripped prematurely from his mother's womb.

'Despair thy charm;
And let the angel whom thou still hast served
Tell thee, Macduff was from his mother's womb
Untimely ripp'd.'

Macbeth realized how falsely the witches had played him but vowed that he would not bow down to anyone. The two continued fighting till Macduff overcame Macbeth and beheaded him.

The battle ended with the tyrant's death, and Malcolm was proclaimed the king of Scotland by all the lords who were invited to his crowning at Scone. He conferred honours upon all those who had sided with him in the battle, signifying that he would be a good and merciful ruler like his late father, Duncan.

Brief Note

Macbeth, written around 1606, is one of the most popular plays by William Shakespeare, and one frequently performed across the world. The character of Macbeth was based on a real king who usurped the throne of Scotland from King Duncan in 1040. Banquo was a friend of the actual Macbeth, and King James I claimed him as an ancestor through the Stuart dynasty.

One reason why *Macbeth* has been performed so prolifically may be because it is Shakespeare's shortest tragedy, less than 2,500 lines. It was first performed at the Globe Theatre in 1606 with the popular actor, Richard Burbage, playing the lead role.

It was rumoured that there was a curse on the play, originally called *The Scottish Play*, as some mishaps and tragedies took place during its production. People even said that if the name *Macbeth* was pronounced in a theatre, the speaker would have to walk three times round in a circle, anti-clockwise, and then utter a swear word or spit.

Another interesting story involved a certain actor, who was considered the worst poet of his times, who played the role of Macbeth, and refused to die at the end of the play. In Disney's *Snow White and the Seven Dwarfs*, the evil queen closely resembled the on-screen persona of Lady Macbeth.

10
THE TEMPEST

THE TEMPEST

10.1: *The Tempest.*
Artist: S.K. Riazul Rahaman.

Characters in the Order of their Appearance

Prospero, the magician and the erstwhile Duke of Milan
Antonio, Prospero's brother and the present Duke of Milan

Deepti Menon

Alonso, the King of Naples
Sebastian, the brother of the King of Naples
Ferdinand, the son of the King of Naples
Miranda, Prospero's daughter
Gonzalo, an elderly counsellor, loyal to Prospero
Ariel, a spirit in bondage to Prospero
The Crew of the Ship
Sycorax, the witch
Caliban, the misshapen son of Sycorax
Stephano, a butler
Trinculo, a court jester

A tumultuous tempest raged at sea, with a ship desperately trying to brave the elements. It was a man-made storm, created by a mighty magician named Prospero. The passengers within the ship were men of importance—Prospero's treacherous brother, Antonio, Alonso, the King of Naples, his brother, Sebastian, his son, Prince Ferdinand and Gonzalo, the trusted adviser to the King of Naples.

On shore, Prospero stood, watching the storm with his daughter, Miranda, whose tender heart wept for the crew. Prospero assured the fifteen-year-old girl that no harm would come to any of them. The time was now ripe to tell her about who she was and how they had come to the island.

"Twelve year since, Miranda, twelve year since,
Thy father was the Duke of Milan and
A prince of power."

As Miranda listened on, rapt, her father revealed how, twelve years ago, he had been the Duke of Milan, a much-loved leader, known for his great knowledge. Prospero had burrowed himself in his books and his secret studies.

'Me, poor man, my library was dukedom large enough.'

He had, thus, left the running of the state to his ambitious brother, Antonio, who slowly, but steadily, devised a plan to depose Prospero, with the help of Alonso, the King of Naples. Soon, he usurped the dukedom of Milan.

Prospero and his three-year-old daughter, Miranda, escaped on a decrepit boat, aided by the loyal Gonzalo, who gave them supplies of food and clothing, and more importantly, some books from Prospero's library that he valued more highly than even his dukedom.

"Knowing I loved my books, he furnish'd me
From mine own library with volumes that
I prize above my dukedom."

They travelled all the way to the island aided by divine providence and since then, it had been their home where he had perfected the art of magic.

Miranda, who had been listening intently, wondered why her uncle had not put them both to death. Prospero explained that his brother was aware of the great love that the people of Milan bore them and hence, he did not want to shed their blood.

Miranda then asked him why he had created the tempest. His reply was that fate had conspired to bring all their enemies together to this shore. As Miranda listened to her father, she suddenly found herself falling asleep, probably due to a charm invoked by him.

The spirit, Ariel, Prospero's servant, appeared and told him of how he had flown about inside the wrecked ship like thunder, lightning and the wind, terrifying everyone within. The crew was put to sleep within the ship, while the others were safely spirited towards the island. Ariel mentioned that he had brought Ferdinand, the prince, to an isolated part of the island.

Prospero was happy with his spirit's good work but told him that there was more to be done. Ariel took the opportunity to remind his master that he had promised to free him of bondage if he served him well. Prospero was annoyed with Ariel's words and harshly reminded him of the pitiful state he had found him in, trapped inside a pine tree, by the dreadful witch, Sycorax. She had borne a misshapen son, Caliban, and died before setting Ariel free. When Prospero arrived at the island, he had heard Ariel's groans and freed him.

> *'What torment did I find you in; thy groans*
> *Did make wolves howl.'*

Prospero threatened to imprison Ariel in an oak tree for twelve years if he grumbled any more. Ariel was chastened and promised to continue doing his master's bidding. Prospero then ordered him to turn into an invisible nymph, only visible to Prospero's eyes.

By now, Miranda had woken up and Prospero and she went to converse with the ungainly Caliban, who spewed curses on them both. Prospero warned him that he would punish him with cramps the whole night. Caliban had a grudge against Prospero who had imprisoned him on the island which had belonged to his mother, Sycorax, and him. Prospero called him ungrateful because, even though Prospero had taught him to speak, Caliban had proved himself unworthy of being around civilized people. He was, hence, imprisoned to a rock, his only task being to fetch wood for his master. Caliban's mocking reply was that since Prospero had taught him to speak, he could now curse with fluency.

> *'You taught me language: and my profit on't*
> *Is, I know how to curse.'*

Ariel made an appearance once again, leading Prince Ferdinand with his music to where Prospero and Miranda stood. When Miranda laid eyes on Ferdinand, she was entranced for she had never seen any man apart from her father and Caliban. She wondered if he were a spirit, and she said to Prospero,

> *'I might call him*
> *A thing divine, for nothing natural*
> *I ever saw so noble.'*

Ferdinand too was smitten by the beautiful lady and he revealed himself as the prince of Naples. Prospero was pleased at the way things were proceeding, but he did not want to make it too easy for the two. Hence, he accused Ferdinand of pretending to be the prince of Naples at which the prince took offence and drew his sword. Prospero put a charm on him so that he could not move.

Miranda pleaded with her father to treat the prince gently. Prospero did not heed her, but, instead, led Ferdinand to where he would stay imprisoned.

Meanwhile, the other shipwrecked persons wandered around, lost and weary. Stephano, a drunken butler, and

Trinculo, an equally drunken court jester, encountered Caliban. They offered him sack, (alcohol) and he turned into their devoted slave. Conspiring to kill Prospero with his help, they plotted to take over the island.

Alonso, the King of Naples, was disconsolate because he believed his son, Ferdinand, had been drowned. As they made desultory conversation, with Gonzalo, their adviser, trying to cheer the king up, Ariel flitted by and put all, except Antonio and Sebastian, to sleep.

The time was ripe for a conspiracy. Antonio suggested that Sebastian should murder his sleeping brother, so that he could take over his kingdom. He assured him that usurping Prospero's dukedom had been the best step he had taken in his life. Sebastian was convinced.

> *'Draw thy sword: one stroke*
> *Hall free thee from the tribute which thou payest:*
> *And I the king shall love thee.'*

Just as they were about to kill both Alonso and Gonzalo, Ariel woke Gonzalo up, shouting 'Awake! Awake!', thus foiling the murderous plan.

Ferdinand was now hefting logs as Prospero had ordered him to. Miranda came in and beseeched him to stop, for it grieved her to see him doing such heavy work. As they conversed and spoke of love, Prospero was an invisible listener. Miranda admitted that she loved Ferdinand and was willing to be his wife. Ferdinand, on his part, told her that he was a prince, and likely to be king as well. Miranda proposed to Ferdinand, who accepted her gladly.

'The very instant that I saw you, did
My heart fly to your service; there resides,
To make me slave to it.'

Prospero was jubilant that things were working out exactly the way he wanted.

Alonso, along with Sebastian, Antonio and Gonzalo, was still searching for his son, hoping against hope that he had survived the tempest. They were all exhausted and suddenly, to their amazement, several strange spirits appeared with a magical banquet. However, before they could feast, the banquet vanished, and Ariel came in the form of a harpy and accused them of having betrayed Prospero by driving him out from Milan with his young daughter. The powers of nature and the sea had taken revenge by drowning Alonso's son.

Prospero, by now, had decided that he had tried Ferdinand enough and he gave his consent to the union of the young lovers. Three goddesses—Iris, Juno and Ceres—performed a betrothal masque for the couple. Ferdinand was so rapt that he wanted to live on the island forever.

'Let me live here ever,
So rare a wonder'd father and a wife
Makes this place Paradise.'

As the magic revelry continued, Prospero suddenly recalled that Caliban had conspired with two others to murder him. He worked himself into a rage which astonished the young couple, and he requested them to go in and leave him alone, adding,

'We are such stuff
As dreams are made on, and our little life
Is rounded with a sleep.'

Ariel, in the meantime, had led Caliban and his co-conspirators, Stephano and Trinculo, a merry dance across prickly briars into a dirty pool. Now they were waiting outside Prospero's cell, drenched, and distracted by a line of glittery clothes that beckoned them enticingly. Caliban insisted that they should commit the murder immediately, but the two drunken men were keener on handling the clothes. Suddenly, a host of spirits, disguised as hunting hounds, bounded onto the scene, and drove the conspirators away as Ariel and Prospero looked on, invisible spectators.

It was now time for Prospero's plans to come to a head. He would no longer need his magical powers.

'But the rough magic
I here abjure… I'll break my staff,
Bury it certain fathoms in the earth,
And deeper than ever did plummet sound
I'll drown my book.'

Ariel had brought all the shipwrecked people to one spot outside his cell. As they walked into the circle that Prospero had drawn, a charm held them captive as Prospero addressed them, revealing himself as the betrayed Duke of Milan. He praised the loyalty of the aged Gonzalo and accused all the others of betraying him. As they stared on in disbelief, Alonso seemed remorseful for the way he had treated Prospero. He offered him his dukedom again, adding that his cup of sorrow was full since he had lost his son, Ferdinand at sea. Prospero's answer to that was that he had also lost a daughter. Alonso cried out in sympathy,

'A daughter?
Oh heavens, that they were living both in Naples,
The king and queen there.'

He could not believe his eyes when he witnessed Ferdinand and Miranda playing a game of chess.

When Miranda saw so many people she exclaimed,

'How beauteous mankind is! Oh, brave new world,
That has such people in't.'

The whole company was happy to see the young couple so much in love. Meanwhile, Ariel had worked his magic and awoken the crew of the ship whom he had put under a spell, and got the ship restored to its seaworthy self. Prospero was so pleased with his faithful spirit that he granted him the freedom that he had been yearning for. Ariel's last task for his master was to ensure favourable winds for their voyage back to Milan.

'My Ariel, chick,
That is thy charge: then to the elements
Be free, and fare thou well!'

Prospero then invited Alonso and company to stay on the island for one more night and hear how he and Miranda had spent the last twelve years. The next day, they would all set sail to Naples where Ferdinand and Miranda would be married, and where Prospero himself would live out the rest of his remaining life. Now that he did not need the powers of his magic anymore, he was ready to abandon it.

For the last time, he ordered Ariel to grant them fair weather for their voyage before he set him free.

Brief Note

The Tempest was one of Shakespeare's last plays, written between 1610 and 1611. It encompassed a larger-than-life canvas, encapsulating a world filled with magic, betrayal, disillusionment, power and freedom, revenge and forgiveness. This play was listed in the First Folio as one of the Bard's first comedies, but it has elements of comedy, tragedy and romance. One interpretation put forth the explanation of the play as a fable of creation and art, with Shakespeare himself as Prospero, the master creator, and Prospero's final renouncement of magic as an indication of Shakespeare bidding adieu to the stage.

The Tempest must have been a challenge to present on stage, with the spectacle of the storm-tossed ship and the shipwreck at the beginning of the play, followed by the masque, which in Renaissance England was a gala at court, replete with entertainment, music, dance, elaborate costumes, and drama. It was set in an era whose culture and society were male-dominated, and there is only one female protagonist in the play, Miranda, who had never seen any man apart from her father, and the ungainly Caliban.

Records say that a performance of the play was staged before King James I on 1st November, 1611. As the play had more music than any of the other plays of Shakespeare, including two songs—'Full Fathom Five' and 'Where the Bee Sucks'—it attracted the attention of composers as well as dramatists.

Prospero is a powerful protagonist who speaks almost one-third of the lines in *The Tempest* and plays the role of a master puppeteer, as he manipulates the lives and actions of all the other characters through magic, even as he orchestrates the action to a fitting finale.

FUN FACTS ABOUT SHAKESPEARE

1. *The Comedy of Errors* is Shakespeare's shortest play. It is only 1,770 lines long.

2. *Hamlet* is his longest play at 4,000 lines, which would have taken three hours onstage.

3. The normal length of an Elizabethan play was two hours, which was just about the time required for the audience to get home before dark. This was because London after dark was filled with peril, and playwrights were aware of that.

4. The reference to witches in *Macbeth* made the play unpopular with audiences. Theatre people were superstitious of uttering the name 'Macbeth' aloud.

5. Portraits of William Shakespeare, especially the famous Chandos portrait, (below) reveal that he wore a gold hoop on his left ear, which in those days, pointed to a Bohemian lifestyle.

6. The concept of copyright did not exist in Shakespeare's time, and to avoid copying, actors often received their lines only when they were on stage. Often, they were given whispered cues just before they were to deliver the lines.

7. Most writers wrote during the day and partied at night. The reason was simpler than expected. Candles were expensive and used rarely, and only during crises. Shakespeare was no different from his contemporaries as far as using candles frugally went.

8. The Globe Theatre was constructed to accommodate people from all walks of life. The poor sat on the ground floor with no seats and no roof or cover to shelter them from the cold, rain or the biting wind. The wealthy sat above in galleries that were covered and far from the madding crowd below.

9. Women were not expected to act. There were no female actors and young boys often played the roles of the women characters in Shakespeare's plays.

10. The longest word in Shakespeare is 'honorificabilitudinitatibus', used in the play *Love's Labour Lost*. It means 'invincible glorious honorableness'.

11. The Bard seemed fascinated by suicide. When counted, the suicides that occurred in his plays numbered thirteen. He referenced birds a whopping 600 times in his plays and mentioned dogs around 200 times.

12. Theatre performances were rather informal with people talking and eating right through the production. In fact, when the audience got tired of the action on stage, they would boo, shout and throw eatables at the unlucky actors.

13. Why did Shakespeare turn to writing sonnets? The plague caused the shutting down of theatres (doesn't

that sound familiar?) and hence, he began writing poetry.

14. And the mother of all facts to end this curious list... Did you realize that William Shakespeare was an anagram of 'I am a weakish speller'? Mind blowing, isn't it?

REFERENCES

The Complete Works of William Shakespeare, Massachusetts Institute of Technology (MIT).

William Shakespeare Biography, Shakespeare Birthplace Trust.

William Shakespeare, Historic UK.

https://www.williamshakespeare.net/

ΛCKNOWLEDGEMENTS

'O Lord that lends me life,
Lend me a heart replete with thankfulness.'

William Shakespeare, *Henry VI*

1. I can never forget my two erudite grandfathers, who propelled me gently into the world of Literature. One would read me classical stories, the other would help me rehearse for my recitation contests till I was word perfect

2. My parents, who blew into me the Literature gene, so dominant that it does not allow me to rest in peace the day I do no writing

3. My sisters, whose lives I turned into a Gothic horror story with my gory tales that gave them sleepless nights

4. My long-suffering husband, who tolerates the Bard only for my sake

5. My daughter, who was the sole Muse to my writing until she gifted us with two tiny Muses, our grandchildren

6. Prasad K., our multi-faceted Art master who encouraged our talented team of students from Hari Sri Vidya Nidhi School to create the illustrations with such finesse and gusto... Vrindha Nair, S.K. Riazul Rahaman, Krishna N.P., Pavithra S. Nair, Pranav Prakash, Manasa Kalyan, Anjali S., Adithya Sujith, Leah Teresa Chakola, Binitta Biffin and Ghanshyam M.

7. My brilliant beta readers, all between the ages of eleven and fifteen. Each gave me nuggets of wisdom which helped me enhance my writing further... Purvaja

Acknowledgements

Yennamaneni, Ananya Gulati, Shreyas Saboo, Ira Kulkarni and Arnav Mahajan from Beyond the Box ably helmed by the inspiring Anupama Dalmia. I must also thank our amazing English teachers, Bindu Sudheesan and Deepa T.R., and our young beta readers from Hari Sri Vidya Nidhi School, Thrissur… Sreedevi S. Menon, Manasa Ramesh, Ananth Ram J., Diya Rose Denny, Saniya K., Niranjana Murali and Aneena J. Kunnath. Last but never least, my heartfelt gratitude to Ananya Nair from Dubai!

8. My online writer friends with whom I have an ongoing contest where we all complete writing challenges even as we burn the midnight oil to catch those deadlines that otherwise tend to whoosh by. They are a formidable army of friends, indeed!

9. My tireless publisher, Dipankar Mukherjee, of Readomania fame and our lovely Editor Sahiba, Indrani Ganguly, both of whom are an immense inspiration, the wind beneath my wings.

DEEPTI MENON
Thrissur, 2023

ABOUT THE AUTHOR

Deepti Menon has always loved the written word. She has published four books, starting with *Arms and the Woman* (Rupa Publishers). *Deeparadhana of Poems* came next, followed by The Shadow Trilogy—*Shadow in the Mirror, Where Shadows Follow* and *Shadows Never Lie,* and *Classic Tales from The Panchatantra* (all by Readomania).

As a freelance journalist in Chennai, she wrote umpteen articles for various publications, and was lucky enough to interview celebrities like Jeffrey Archer, Ruskin Bond and many others, including film stars, business tycoons and politicians.

Deepti has always enjoyed writing thriller short stories and has been published in around twenty anthologies, including *Unkahi: The Unsung* (Part 1) along with other noteworthy writers. She is presently working on three manuscripts which, she hopes, will soon see the light of day. Her latest book, *Defying Destiny: Nalini Chandran—A Life Sketch* (Logos Books), is a life sketch on Ms. Nalini Chandran, her mother who is a renowned educationist.

Deepti has always loved the world of Literature, and remains star-struck by the writings of Shakespeare. This book is an attempt to demystify his plays for young minds, by metamorphosing them into crisp short stories, peppered with actual quotes from the original.

Deepti firmly believes in the Paula Hawkins quote:

"Stay faithful to the stories in your head."

That is exactly what she does as a writer.

About the Author

Deepti Menon can be found at:
https://www.facebook.com/deepti.menon.98
https://twitter.com/deepsmenon_7
https://www.instagram.com/deepties_7/
https://deepties.blogspot.com/

READO JUNIOR

www.ingramcontent.com/pod-product-compliance
Lightning Source LLC
LaVergne TN
LVHW091503170726
843492LV00001B/328